Praise for Elizabeth Engstrom's work

On The Itinerant:

"An often-thrilling speculative tale that will keep readers engaged." —*Kirkus Reviews*

"Anyone interested in stories of post-apocalyptic survival and transformation will find *The Itinerant* more intriguing, holding a deeper message about humanity's objectives and survival, than most genre reads."
—D. Donovan, Senior Reviewer, *Midwest Book Review*

"Engstrom is an expert at suspense, with more than a dozen creepy novels and short story collections to her credit. *The Itinerant*, though, offers more than breathtaking chills and thrills as it works its way to a final spiritual resolution." —Bob Keefer, *The Eugene Weekly*

On Baggage Check:

"The author is so deft at creating interesting, 3D characters that I was instantly hooked into Sweetann's plight (yes, Sweetann). Even the bad guys have depth and lives beyond the story. This is not a typical thriller which makes it much more interesting than the average shoot 'em up, and Sweetann is not a typical heroine. A guaranteed fun time." —*Christina Lay, author of Death is a Star*, editor at Shadow Spinners Books

On Black Leather:

...a darkly seductive page-turner by a writer who knows how to put the erotic thrill into a thriller.
—*DarkEcho*

...an artfully written and highly recommended erotic and psychological suspense from first page to last.
—*Midwest Book Review*

On **Suspicions:**

"This is where she's at her best." —*Locus*

"A harrowing and suspenseful anthology filled with superbly crafted short stories about love, death, sex, and crossing the River Styx. Dark humor courses through these dramatic and sometimes horrific tales, in this blood-curdling anthology that leaves a fearsome chill in one's spine long after the last page has been turned. *Suspicions* is strongly recommended reading for those that prefer their literary entertainment with a decided flair for the unexpected." —*Midwest Book Review*

"A spooky collection of tales." —*Publishers Weekly*

"A hefty, genre-crossing pie spiced with images capable of snagging the imagination." —*Booklist*

"Elizabeth Engstrom has selected twenty-five (four original to the collection) stories from the past twenty years of writing that reveal her as a suspicious sort. But then, aren't we all? We all suspect the unknown, death, sex, and "friends, family, love, work, technology, the government, and everything else." It's just that Elizabeth Engstrom can take her lack of trust and craft fine fiction from it. Like many fine writers, Engstrom's stories are across all genres. Some can be termed sf, others as mystery or fantasy or horror, still others are simply "fiction." A few are light and humorous. Most are quietly dark, slightly skewed, angled toward that indescribable place just at the edge of shadow. All are worth reading. Many are worth pondering. By the end, at least one suspicion will definitely be confirmed: Elizabeth Engstrom is one of the best. No doubts." —*Cemetery Dance*

On **York's Moon:**

"*York's Moon* is so absorbing and unusual that you'll almost miss how beautifully written it is—almost. Elizabeth Engstrom's mesmerizing and unique style will draw you into a world of mystery, violence and heroic struggle. Ultimately, this story celebrates the uplifting power of the human spirit. Do not miss it." —Susan Wiggs, bestselling author of *Marrying Daisy Bellamy*

"With quirky, engaging characters, *York's Moon* is as much about understanding the human condition as solving a murder mystery. I cannot imagine anyone but Liz Engstrom writing this fine novel." —Terry Brooks, author of the *Shannara* series

"This book is most certainly not what you would call your average mystery. In fact, there are many facets of inspirational fiction, melancholy drama, and threads of romance scattered throughout, that mix in extremely well with the murder mystery that this novel focuses on." —*Once upon a Romance*

On **The Northwoods Chronicles:**

"Engstrom, a skilled horror fiction stylist whose novels include the biographical *Lizzie Borden* (1991), here gives us a deliciously creepy collection of interrelated stories. White Pines Junction is a quaint, sparsely populated tourist town that, along with its many outdoors-oriented charms, harbors some very dark secrets. Aside from a little-publicized history of hometown thugs and serial killers, the town trades deaths with its garbage dump on a one-for-one citizen-rat basis and hosts a motel whose residents' nighttime reveries become frighteningly true. Perhaps most disturbing of all, the town is tormented by an epidemic of mysteriously disappearing children. In one story, a preacher's pregnant wife becomes increasingly psychotic until an unearthly force literally steals the child from her womb. In another, a harried wife finds the grisly means to dispose of her troublesome husband behind the soon-to-be-remodeled walls of her kitchen. Engstrom's chilling scenarios will haunt readers' dreams for days." —*Booklist*

"Dark fantasy writer Engstrom (*Black Leather*) starts on familiar ground, but rapidly turns this 'novel in stories' into a genre-blending exploration of love, aging, grief and sacrifice. In Vargas County, children under 12 occasionally vanish, but the locals have long viewed this as a tithe taken by the town in exchange for the happiness of the other residents. This theme is explored directly in stories like 'House Odds,' in which real estate agent Julia has to decide if her grandchildren would be in greater danger in town or away with their drunken father. Other tales merely use the disappearances as a backdrop, such as 'Skytouch Fever,' in which aging Sadie Katherine is forced to choose between her steadfast beau and a rakish visitor, and the wittily ironic thriller

'One Quiet Evening in the Wax Museum.' Fast-paced, melancholy and beautiful, the overarching narrative binds a collection of good stories into a superb if unconventional novel." —*Publishers Weekly*

"*The Northwoods Chronicles* conjured up in me the same excitement and wonder I felt when I read Ray Bradbury's *The Martian Chronicles*. I was taken far away...inside my own heart, my fears, my hopes. I set it down to tend to life; forgot where I put it; got anxious just like Recon John when the monkey jawbone went missing. I finished it, but it's not over: I've been gifted with a life in a strange new world, not without its shadows, and the glimmer of weird on the water. This one is a keeper, and I'm one of its kept. Brava, Elizabeth Engstrom." —Nancy Holder, author of *Son of the Shadows*

"To read Elizabeth Engstrom is to be guided by the sure hand of an accomplished writer whose stories have the power to transfer readers to places both real and surreal. We believe in the unbelievable, marvel at worlds created between dream and reality, and reach for all that transcends the limits of our imagination." —Gail Tsukiyama, author of *The Street of a Thousand Blossoms*

"From the ominous opening to the soaring conclusion, these braided stories – subtle and spooky and smart – will keep the reader spellbound. The Northwoods is a scary place to live, but in Ms. Engstrom's hands, it's a fabulous visit." —Karen Joy Fowler, author of *The Jane Austen Book Club*

"Were he still alive, Rod Serling would like Engstrom's book. Presented separately, each of her narratives would make a great segment of the classic "Twilight Zone" television program so popular in the 1960s. Taken together — and given Serling's absence among us — they give us another way to hold a book in our hands that gives our spines a tingle and makes us wonder if Serling is really so far away after all." —*Eugene Register Guard*

On **Lizzie Borden:**

"Marvelous stuff. The pressures on Lizzie were vivid and completely real. You know, I think I'd have killed him myself..."—Mercedes Lackey, author of the *Heralds of Valdemar* series

"Every door in the Borden house is metaphorically locked, and each room holds the terrible secrets of the occupant... Engstrom [moves] the reader inexorably toward the anticipated savage denouement."—*Publishers Weekly*

"Elizabeth Engstrom has woven a fascinating tale of a lonely, tormented and frustrated young woman."—*Rocky Mountain News*

"A real page-turner and white-knuckler. The tension mounts without letup."—*Maui News*

"Engstrom crafts a character with motivation, mental confusion and smoldering resentment, a woman who could stand unblinking in a shower of blood as she bludgeoned her parents to death."—*Ogden Standard Examiner*

On **Lizard Wine**:

"*Lizard Wine* is the book your mother warned you about, sleek, nasty, perfectly focused, smart as hell, absolutely convincing, and utterly single-minded. This novel wants to buy you a drink, whisper in your ear, coax you into a dark room and there seriously mess you up. Because Elizabeth Engstrom is a magnificently talented writer, her novel not only actually does these things, it leaves you grateful for the experience. *Lizard Wine* is the kind of book which enlarges and enriches the genre of the thriller."—Peter Straub, author of *Ghost Story*

"...*Lizard Wine* is a book that will make your skin crawl."—John Saul, author of *The Blackstone Chronicles*

"...hard! Should carry a health warning: Just reading this could leave you bruised..."—Brian Lumley, author of the *Necroscope* series

"Excruciating suspense!"—Bryce Courtenay, author of *The Power of One*

"*Lizard Wine* is a disturbing vintage... With a true literary voice, Elizabeth Engstrom details the madness of human relationships... It is as if Franz Kafka, Tom Robbins and Shirley Jackson collaborated on a story which only Engstrom could write. A brilliant, page-turning read."—Douglas Clegg, author of *The Children's Hour*

"Reading *Lizard Wine* is like sitting in a snowbound car with three very dangerous men and three vulnerable (yet-no-less-dangerous) young women, and watching in thrall as the balance of power trades hands through the night. Elizabeth Engstrom involves her readers equally with the pitiful and the pitiless, and as the sun rises on the living and the dead, we close this novel reminded that we can make our lives, or our lives can make us. *Lizard Wine* is a dark, rough draught, but it goes down as smooth as the grit will allow—and its after-effects are potent and lingering."—Tim Lucas, author of *Throat Sprockets*

"Supertaut storytelling..."—*Kirkus Reviews*

"I often stopped with a low mental whistle of awe at Engstrom's seamless style..."—*DarkEcho*

"...Deliverance meets Misery..."—*The Fiction Addiction*

"...Don't read this book alone at night."—*Eugene Register Guard*

"...The message of *Lizard Wine* is clear. This could be anybody. This could be you."—*AmericaOnline*

On When Darkness Loves Us:

"Engstrom's genre masterwork, comprising two harrowing novellas, exemplifies the rarest breed of horror stories: as tender as they are unsettling, as tragic as they are bloody, these are monster tales that sweep the reader along on currents of pained feeling rather than on the familiar beats of the ol' Creature Feature." —*Los Angeles Review of Books*

"Finding the light when swamped in darkness is never an easy thing. *When Darkness Loves Us* is a collection of two novellas from Elizabeth Engstrom. One story follows a young farm girl as she is engulfed by an underworld and yearns to escape, and an old woman who is facing the monsters of her past. Two engaging stories make *When Darkness Loves Us* quite a pick." —*Midwest Book Review*

Citations

IFD Publishing, P.O. Box 41281, Eugene, Oregon 97404 U.S.A.
www.ifdpublishing.com

Unrequited Loss

Cover art, copyright © 2025 Alan M. Clark

ISBN: 979-8-9852827-9-5

Books by Elizabeth Engstrom

When Darkness Loves Us
Black Ambrosia
Nightmare Flower
Lizzie Borden
Lizard Wine
The Alchemy of Love
Suspicions
Black Leather
Candyland
The Northwoods Chronicles
York's Moon
Baggage Check
How to Write a Sizzling Sex Scene
Benediction Denied
Divorce by Grand Canyon
The Itinerant
Unrequited Loss

Word by Word (editor, with John Tullius)
Imagination Fully Dilated (co-editor)
Imagination Fully Dilated vol. II (editor)
Dead on Demand (editor)
Pronto! Writings from Rome (editor, with John Tullius)
Ship's Log: Writings at Sea (editor, with John Tullius)
Lies and Limericks (editor, with John Tullius)
Mota 9: Addiction (editor)

Unrequited Loss

A collection of short fiction

by

Elizabeth Engstrom

IFD Publishing

Acknowledgements

This collection of short fiction spans a considerable length of time, time spent teaching the writing of ghost stories to a wonderful group of writers, time spent in the company of an amazing writing group, time spent in the company of writers of like mind, if not temperament. It is to each of these people that I owe my thanks for their intuition, their brave appraisals, their dedication to the process, and to their willingness. Most of all, I'm grateful to count among my friends many former students who continue to surprise and inspire me in ways they can never imagine. I am awash in gratitude for those who continue to read my work.

Dedication

To Al Cratty, always and forevermore.

Table of Contents

Suki's Garden

Suki pulled her nightshirt up past her knees and felt the ridges of bumps that ran up the front of her thigh. They were still there. Little rows of bumps. Bigger than even an hour ago when she got into a fresh nightshirt. She wouldn't be able to keep it a secret much longer.

Nor did she want to. She wanted everybody to know that she'd been called, but she didn't want to leave the school, and as soon as she showed the headmistress what was growing on her skin, they'd make her leave.

She slipped out of her narrow bed and walked quietly on the balls of her feet past three sleeping girls to Juju's bed, lifted up the blanket and sheet and slipped in next to her warm friend.

"Juju," Suki whispered. "Wake up."

"What?" A sleepy Juju moved over to accommodate her friend. "What are you doing?"

"I got my calling."

Juju's eyes grew wide in the darkness, reflecting what little light seeped in from the hallway. "Oh, no." She grabbed Suki and hugged her tightly. "Don't tell. Don't go. I'll die without you here!" She buried her face in Suki's nightshirt and began to sob.

"You won't die, little sister," Suki whispered, her emotions a confusing combination of excitement, dread and sadness. "Besides, it's going to happen to everyone. You might be next. We might see each other out in the—"

The door opened, and the headmistress stood silhouetted in the hall light. Both girls froze in fear. Suki, the offender, tried to make herself as small as possible in Juju's bed, hoping the headmistress would think there was only one girl there.

No chance. The woman's shoes clicked on the concrete floor and stopped at the foot of Juju's bed.

Suki looked up defiantly.

"Back to your own bed," the headmistress said, her voice harsh even in a whisper.

"Not tonight," Suki replied.

Even in this dim light, Suki could see the surprise on the old woman's face. Perhaps nobody had ever defied her before. Without another word, she turned and left the dormitory. There would be hell to pay, but for now, Suki held her best friend close and tried to imagine what life held for her outside the walls of their school.

~ ~ ~

In the morning, when Suki was called to the Headmistress' office, she raised her skirt and showed the rows of vegetables beginning to sprout on her thighs and was dismissed to go back to classes. At dinner, she'd had no appetite and others had to take food from her plate so she wouldn't be further penalized for not eating. In the washroom, the whole dormitory was subdued as well. Those who spoke did so quietly about Kitzie, who had that very morning received her calling as a weaver and sent immediately after lunch to the creamery. Suki's stomach continued to boil with worry and dread.

The creamery.

None of the girls had ever returned from the creamery. It stood high on a knoll at the edge of the school grounds. The high walls that surrounded the school seemed to start and stop at the Creamery, a squat stone building that straddled the stream and kept milk products, eggs and cheese cool. Once a day, Cook went to the creamery to fetch the day's rations, but now and then another girl was sent, one who had received her calling, and was never heard from again.

Rumor had it that a demon lived in the creamery and had his way with the girls, took them to his lair in the underworld. This, of course, was forbidden talk, which made it all the more plausible to the girls.

Why had Suki not been sent to the creamery?

Before bedtime, she showed the other girls the vegetables growing on both her thighs, and now little bumps of ridges had begun on her forearms. On the left thigh, clearly could be seen the lacy tops of a row of carrots, the dark red foliage of beets, long spires of onions and dots of green heads of lettuce. The girls oohed and aahed, and Suki forgot her dread of the future for a moment while reveling in the feeling of being special. Rarely did any of the girls get to actually witness another's calling, as they were dispatched so quickly upon discovery.

"I don't think there's a demon," Juju said, holding back the tears.

"But there is," stupid Cassie said. "Lots of girls have seen it. Horrible, it is, with its skull showing black through its scalp, burned out eyes and long fingernails. It's horrible, it smells all the way to forever, and it takes those..." Suddenly, the little twit realized that Suki was likely the next to go and turned away.

Suki dropped down her nightshirt to cover her thighs and went into the bedroom. She and Juju got into bed together, unwilling to sleep alone on what might be her last night alive, daring the headmistress to do anything about it.

"What's the purpose?" she whispered after the lights went out. "Juju, why would they school us if we are only to be food for the demon?"

"The demon can't be real," Juju said, then began to cry. Suki held her and rocked her until they both drifted off to sleep.

~ ~ ~

At breakfast, Cook came out of the kitchen, and the room went silent.

"I need you to fetch a round of cheese from the creamery," Cook said to Suki.

Suki nodded, finished chewing, set her fork down, folded her napkin and got up from the table.

"I'm going with you," Juju said.

Cook put a restraining hand on the girl's arm. "I asked Suki to go."

"It's okay," Suki said, smiled a tentative smile at Juju and then at the other girls around the room whose breakfasts had surely turned to dust in their mouths. She handed her plate and cup to Cook, and then bravely left the cafeteria.

Moving steadily so she wouldn't give in to her pounding heart and the terror that threatened to suck the strength out of her legs, Suki went out the front door of the school and then through the sad, rocky patch where Old Max, the maintenance man, had endeavored to grow some vegetables. For the first time, she could see how easy it would be to improve the soil, how they could feed the worms and microbes in the soil to enrich it, how digging out the rocks would make everything easier. Suki had seen this sad attempt at gardening from the classroom window a million times, but only now could she hear the soil, the stunted and tortured plants, listen to their cries for nutrition and water. Old Max knew nothing about gardening and neither had she...until now.

She wanted to stop and pull a weed whose roots were strangling a sorry tomato plant that would never produce anything but hard little green knots, not the big, red, juicy, delicious fruit that came into her mind when she looked at that plant's potential. A tear dripped off her lower lid and landed on a ravaged cabbage that immediately plumped up and held its leaves up for more. Suki envisioned row upon row of happy, bright and healthy vegetables growing in rich loam— loam the students and faculty could make themselves. She knew how to call the worms. She knew how to dig deeply into the soil and make room for roots to expand; she could see the whole hillside cultivated with fresh, crisp, delicious produce.

Too late.

Her mission was to retrieve a round of cheese for the noontime meal, and the path was straight ahead. Perhaps nothing would happen at the creamery. Perhaps she would be allowed to enter, pick up a heavy round and return with it, and then she and the headmistress could plan the new garden plot and with Old Max as her helper, they could grow delicious, nutritious food for the entire school.

With a sigh of regret, she walked away from the school for the first time ever. She always thought that she would have a great feeling of freedom outside the school walls, but the worn path to the creamery took away all her joy. She walked dutifully up the path toward the low stone building, the only other structure within the tall stone walls.

At the weathered wooden door, she paused and turned for one last glimpse of the only home she had ever known.

As she did, the front door of the school opened, and Juju dashed through.

"No! Juju, go back!"

"I'm going with you," Juju said, all out of breath. She arrived at the door to the creamery, perspiration glistening on her forehead.

Suki felt much braver with her friend at her side. "All right then, if you're sure."

"I'm sure."

Together, they turned and waved at the little faces in the school windows, then Suki opened the creamery door, and they stepped into the cool dim interior.

Water burbled up through a fissure in the rocks, and on both sides of the stream were shelves heavily laden with bottles of milk, cream, and waxed rounds of different colors of cheese. A slab of bacon moldered quietly in the farthest corner.

Relief weakened Suki's knees. "See?" she said. "Cook just wanted—"

But before she could finish the sentence, a door opened in the back of the creamery.

Juju screamed and turned to hide her face from the demon.

But it was no demon, it was just a woman, dressed in dungarees, carrying a shovel. "Come, Suki."

Suki squinted against bright sunlight, sunlight like she'd never seen before, and fertile fields, plowed and ready for the special gift she brought to bear. To the left was a juvenile forest that looked like Rachel, and down in the valley, she could see a lovely little town with the fingerprints of other of her friends who had gone before.

Had no one from the school ever thought to look over the wall?

"Is there a demon?" Juju cried, cowering in the corner.

Suki looked up into the kind eyes of the woman who held the door. "No," she said. "No demon."

She took the shovel that was handed to her and walked down the hill, ready to start planting.

The Cure

Patricia took the box from the UPS guy and leaned the heavy front door closed. The box was addressed with her mother's distinctive handwriting, but she'd said nothing about sending a gift. The box wasn't particularly heavy, as if she'd sent a load of books, nor was it remarkably light. Patricia carried it to the kitchen and set it on the table, then got a sharp knife from the drawer and cut the tape that bound the cardboard seams.

A thin mist escaped as she opened the first flap, and Patricia knew exactly what her mother had sent.

An envelope sat on top of the familiar wooden box. Patricia reached for it first, her warm fingers making trails in the thin coating of frost on the lid.

"I wanted to destroy this evil thing," her mother's handwriting had made thick dark impressions in the half sheet of her personal stationery, "but your father wouldn't let me."

Patricia set that angry note aside and turned her attention to the small piece of folded paper that had been in the envelope with her mother's note. Her name was written on the outside, in her grandmother's thin, spidery hand. Patricia unfolded the paper.

"This will become the test of your lifetime, child," the note said. "It was for me. Choose wisely. I will love you forever. —Nani."

So her parents had been cleaning out the old family mansion. Finally. Nani, Patricia's father's mother, had died almost six months ago, but her parents had been too busy to make the trip down to Savannah to get the old house ready to sell. Patricia had wanted to go immediately, had wanted to attend her grandmother's funeral, had wanted to be in the old house, surrounded by her grandmother's things, but her health was so poor she couldn't manage it. She could barely manage to pull the cold wooden box from its shipping carton with her twisted, arthritic hands.

She opened the clasp on the lid and lifted the frosted top on its little piano hinge. Cold mist swirled inside the box and floated up and out, down the sides, across the table and down to the floor.

"Thank you, Nani," she said. "Oh, praise God." She plunged her red and swollen-knuckled hands into the soothing cold, then lifted her face to the sky as she felt the hot inflammation soak away. It felt like icy cold pudding, only dry. The pain in her knuckles receded instantly, and a few moments later, she knew they had returned to normal size, her fingers straightened out, and it all felt so good it was like scratching an itch from the inside. "Thank you, Nani, thank you," she said over and over again. When she felt that the work had been done, she pulled out her hands and found them to look exactly as a normal forty-two-year-old woman's hands ought to look. Not crippled up, swollen, bent and painful, but with straight fingers and normal knuckles. She flexed them, made fists, ran them over the carved contours of the old box, picked up a spoon from the countertop and twirled it between her fingers. Magic. Beyond magic. Miracle.

"I will love you forever too," she whispered.

She spent the rest of the day doing things a normal person does with normal hands. She dug into the spare bedroom closet and found some old embroidery she had abandoned a dozen years ago and took a couple of stitches with the rusty needle. She found a scarf she'd had to stop knitting, picked it up and giddily knit a couple of rows. She showered and let her fingers comb through her freshly-washed hair. She had dexterity again. No pain. She picked up a pen the way a normal person does, the way she used to, and wrote out her shopping list with a flourish. She used a manual can opener to open Rex's cat food.

It wasn't until after she had gone to bed, letting her smooth, normal hands glide effortlessly and pain free over the sheets and silken comforter, that she remembered the note her grandmother had sent. What kind of a test could this wonderful gift be? It was a gift in the greatest sense of the word; she had an obligation to share it, didn't she?

But Nani hadn't.

Why not? Why hadn't her grandmother shared this healing gift with her, when Nani knew she was in such pain and ill health?

"I forgive you, Nani," she whispered. "But I'll be more generous. A gift is to be shared."

Too excited to sleep, Patricia got out of bed, put on her robe, and turned on the light so she could watch her nimble fingers tie the sash into a beautiful bow. Then she went to the kitchen where mist seeped out of the box and pooled on the floor.

She opened it, fanned away the condensation, reached in, and pulled out the lightest fabric she had ever seen. It was like liquid when in the box, but like fabric when pulled out, cool to the touch but not cold. It looked like lace but had a good heft to it. It shimmered a light gray and smelled like Nani. Patricia wrapped it around her shoulders like a shawl and a peace enshrouded her soul. Warmed from the inside, she went back to bed and dreamed of her beloved grandmother, smiling and nodding, smiling and nodding.

While her first thought in the morning was to loan the amazing fabric to her best friend Denise, who was undergoing surgery to remove a malignancy from her liver in the next few days, she speculated that this was too obvious a use for its healing powers, and perhaps that was the riddle in the note her grandmother had sent. She needed to think through very carefully whatever she did with this gift. It had to be worthy of her grandmother's trust in her. She would wait and see about Denise. Perhaps Denise had a lesson to learn. Patricia had learned much in her illnesses; had she been given the gift of a cure too early, she might have missed the wisdom that sickness can bring.

Every night she slept with the strange scarf wrapped around her neck and shoulders. Every morning, she woke up renewed and refreshed—healed in ways she hadn't even known she needed healing. Her teeth had become straighter, whiter. Her skin smoothed out and took on a youthful glow. Her hair thickened and lengthened. Her nails grew out strong instead of brittle and yellowed. She stood taller, her knees and hips no longer aching. Fat melted from her until she fit in clothes she hadn't worn in twenty years.

She put the fabric back in its box before she dressed for the day, and while it seemed warm and comforting as she wore it, it began to exude that strange mist as soon as it left her touch, and she could feel the aching in her hands waiting to return.

She remembered seeing this fabric on the foot of her grandmother's bed, pooled like a small gray slice of dry ice, quietly misting. She'd never been allowed to touch it. "The essence of your grandfather," is all Nani would say about it. Grandfather had been a medium, and Mother sneered that it had been made by a voodoo queen, woven from the ectoplasm that oozed from him while in trance. But Patricia's father had pooh-poohed such nonsense.

She didn't know what it was, but it was like nothing she had ever known before.

Two weeks went by. Three, four. Still, she hadn't called her father, nor had she heard that they'd returned home, van packed with Nani's treasures. She didn't care. She barely thought about them. She was consumed with the idea that she had to pass along Nani's gift. She had no children, no nieces or nephews. Denise had her surgery, and they discovered that the cancer had spread throughout her. More lessons for Denise to learn, so Patricia didn't offer her the use of the healing gift.

Perhaps she should offer it to one of her enemies. Isn't that what Jesus would do? Who did she know—who did she hate—that needed to be healed?

What a delicious olive branch to offer. What a way to turn the other cheek.

What a wise decision.

There was only one such person on her list. Melinda Hightower. Melinda High and Mighty Hightower. Melinda Nose in the air, better than anybody else, and you bloody well better know it, Hightower. Patricia had heard that Melinda had had a breast implant burst and silicone was cruising through her blood stream, in spite of all the surgeons' efforts to scrape it off her ribs, and it was slowly poisoning her to death. A long, slow, ugly, painful death.

What if Patricia just showed up on her doorstep with the cure? What would Miss Hightower think of Patricia then? Would she apologize for being such a nasty bitch since grade school? Would she start inviting Patricia to her classy fund-raising events and maybe even out to luncheon with her and her fine lady friends?

Maybe. And maybe Patricia would kindly, gently, and very graciously decline. She would not allow Melinda Hightower to repay her kindness, no matter how she might beg. This is a gift that required no payment.

Patricia paused as she dialed Melinda's phone number.

Is this what Nani would do?

Yes. This is exactly the type of selfless act that Nani was famous for.

She finished dialing.

"Melinda? This is Patricia King. May I trouble you for a moment of your time?"

"Patricia who?" came the snotty voice.

"Patricia King. I'm sure you'll remember me when you see me. We went to school together."

"And this is about...?"

"Your health," Patricia said. "I heard about your troubles, and I think I might have something that would help you."

Silence on the other end of the phone. Then, warily. "Okay. Come over then." And she hung up.

Patricia wrapped the soft, light scarf around her neck and drove the two miles up the hill to the enormous house where Melinda Hightower lived with the money she had sucked out of her ex-husband's bank account. Patricia pulled up into the big circular drive and parked, her bent and dusty little Corolla looking quite out of place next to Melinda's Bentley.

What I have, money can't buy, she thought smugly to herself, walked up to the front door and rang the bell.

The thin, wan, waif of a gray-haired woman who answered the door bore no resemblance to the vibrant Melinda Hightower that Patricia knew as a pillar of local society. She would never have recognized the woman had it not been for her eyes, dark black and still sharp, if sunken into the hollows of her face. "What is it?" she demanded.

"I...I called you," Patricia stammered, filled with inadequacies, even as she glowed with perfect health in the face of this sickly woman. "I have something to help you heal."

"Yeah?" Melinda said, without opening the door or inviting her in. "What do you think you have that all my doctors don't? And, more importantly, what's it going to cost me?"

Patricia stared into the woman's suspicious eyes and had a bad feeling that if she took the scarf from around her neck and wrapped it around Melinda Hightower's neck that she would never see it again.

She couldn't bear the thought.

And yet... this was the course of action she had decided upon. This was the noble use to which she would put her grandmother's generous gift. To make a better life for this mean spirited, nasty, inhumane piece of crap. She better goddamn well appreciate it.

"May I come in?" Patricia asked.

"I guess," Melinda said, and stepped back.

Once inside the cavernous hall, Patricia slowly unwrapped the scarf from around her own neck. She had to strain against her better judgment to wrap that beautiful bit of magical cloth around Melinda Hightower's scrawny neck, but as soon as she did, Melinda's face changed.

"Oooh," she said.

Patricia stepped back, but kept Melinda within arm's reach, just in case she tried to make a run for it.

"Oh," Melinda said, her eyes wide with wonder. "I can feel it."

Indeed, the roots of Melinda's hair began to turn brown, and Patricia realized that her gift was going to make Melinda young and beautiful again. She'd regain her status as society's golden girl, this time with the added bonus of a miraculous recovery from the brink of death.

Patricia was sorry she had come. She reached for the shawl, but Melinda took a step backward. "No," she said. "Not yet, please not yet."

"It's mine," Patricia said. "I was going to make it a gift to you, but you're too nasty to live. I want it back." Clearly, Melinda had learned nothing, gained no wisdom from her illness. This was all a terrible mistake.

"Please," Melinda said, and grabbed it with both hands.

The scarf tightened around her neck. Melinda pulled at it, but Patricia could see the tendrils that she thought had been fringe began to knot together and pull itself tighter and tighter.

Melinda began to choke, her face turning red, and then blue. She reached out for Patricia, eyes beseeching, but Patricia took a step back. Yes. This was more like it. *This* was the proper reward for Melinda's behavior. The scarf knew it, even if Patricia did not.

Moments later, Melinda Hightower, queen of greed and all that is ugly, lay small and vacant, on the cold marble floor of her foyer.

Patricia gently reached down to retrieve the scarf. Its tendrils reached up to her, crawled up her arm and wound itself around her neck.

Was it her fault that the scarf knew better than she did the way to cure Melinda Hightower?

As she drove back home, she thought of several other people who might need the use of her new scarf.

The world was a mess, she decided, and she was the one with the cure.

Deep Into the Darkness Peering

This piece was my contribution to an anthology of stories that imagined the completion of Edgar Allan Poe's unfinished story "The Lighthouse".

Edgar dropped the pen upon the open book in despair. He was beyond frustration. Frustration would have had him fling the pen to the wall, there to lose its reservoir of ink upon the wallpaper and make work for Virginia. Again. No, the pen just slipped through fingers that had held it poised over the page, motionless for an hour or more as he searched in vain for the word. The right word. The perfect word.

It had fled without ever having been recognized.

Weary, with cramped fingers and slumping shoulders, he hung his head for the briefest of moments, and then stood up, knowing full well what had interfered with his thoughts. There would be a dinner this evening, and he was required to attend. The anticipation of this dreaded event was enough to put him off his work for a week. How he longed for solitude. How he would happily give all he owned, all he was, for a month upon a desolate shore, with nothing to keep him company but the sound of the ocean itself. There to taste the salt, to smell the wind, to hear the jealous rage of gulls and storms.

But that was not to be. Instead, his torment was to be with a wife who adored him, a wife who doted on him, even when all he desired was for her to busy herself elsewhere. And a social calendar! The anguish was exquisite.

Moreover, his disappointment escalated in that he hadn't written, because his reward was not deserved. He'd promised himself that if he filled the page with his inner suffering, he would reward himself with the last of the brandy. That anticipated taste on the tip of his tongue, that phantom flavor consumed his consciousness until there were no words to come through the pen, excepting those describing the dark fruity liquid. And he had spent way too many pages describing his love affair with brandy to write any more. He had exhausted all the adjectives.

He stretched his back and neck, then went to the cabinet in the corner. The bottle was there, patient as evil, and Edgar grabbed it by its throat and pulled the cork. He didn't know which he loathed more: himself or his wicked alcoholic mistress. He put his lips to the mouth of the bottle, and felt sick at the way they squirmed around the glass opening of their own volition, his tongue probing the dry, crusty flavors of the neck, his nose tuned to its fragrance, and then he tipped it up, and liquid heaven poured across his tongue and down his throat to settle in a complacent, smoldering fire in his stomach.

When the bottle was empty, he poured a short glass of water into it, swished that around and drank the rinse water.

Then he walked back to his desk, picked up the pen and flung it against the wall.

"I cannot work under such conditions!" he yelled at no one.

As he knew she would, Virginia came quietly through the study door. "May I get you something?" she asked in her soft voice.

"No," he said, tender with the good woman who had only his best interests at heart. He sank back into his chair, bottle dropping to the floor, unable to even thank her for her concern. "No," he said again. "Nothing." His self-loathing knew no bounds.

She left as soundlessly as she had come in.

There was another bottle of the same brand in the cabinet. He had purchased the two of them when his check from the newspaper came, and he justified the expense with the thought of visitors, but of course no visitors ever came to their house; no one was ever invited. He craved his solitude. But on the off chance that some would happen by, he purchased an extra bottle of brandy.

And now it stood, like a beacon in the darkness of his soul, beckoning him to finish his work so it could light his way to that liquid peace that comforted him in a way his wedding bed could never.

He felt completely at sea.

At sea. The brandy as beacon. The solitude.

The spark lit in his mind, flared, and then like a match, threatened to sputter out. He fetched his pen from the floor and returned to the desk, turned over a fresh page, and wrote *"Jan. 1, 1796. This day—my first on the light-house—I will make this entry in my Diary, as agreed on with..."* with...he glanced down at the empty bottle on the floor. DeGrat Brandy. *"...DeGrat. As regularly as I can keep the journal, I will..."* goddamn dinner parties! *"...but there's no telling what may happen to a man all alone as I am—"* his concentration was interrupted by a coughing spasm, and he was impatient to get the words on paper while he had them at his disposal. As soon as it passed, he resumed. *"—I may get sick, or worse..."*

When he had filled not one page, but two, he set the pen in the fold of the book and rubbed his cramped hand, then ran his hands through his hair. He'd been wrong. He'd been trying to stay away from the brandy while he wrote, using it as a reward. As a farmer might use a carrot to lure an ass. Instead, he *needed* it to write. As soon as he had a swallow of the DeGrat, he had inspiration. The brandy was his muse as well as his reason to live. How he hated it. How he loved it. He was imprisoned within that brown glass, and the resulting vision of his world was warped and dark.

He was inside the bottle. He was within the beacon. He was in his solitude, inside the light-house. Alone. Total solitude. No dinner parties, no meddling, well-meaning wife, no spousal expectations.

Heaven. A dark heaven, to be sure.

He rewarded himself by opening the fresh bottle with shaking hands and drinking long. Then he corked it and went to his bed to dream of cylindrical walls and uncertain seas, a life and career built on capturing illusions on paper.

"Edgar, get up. You must dress."

Edgar opened his eyes and took in the vision of his wife at her dressing table, brushing her hair. "I'm not going."

"You must. Your publisher will be there."

"I'll tell him I was working on a piece for which he will pay me a pauper's wage."

"You may tell him that yourself if you wish. Come along now. We must leave soon."

Edgar lay watching his wife while she twisted her glossy hair and pinned it. He deserved no such creature. He was unsuitable for marriage. He had habits, appetites, disgusting practices that he cared not to remedy, and instead, by marrying his wonderful but homely cousin Virginia to keep her from spinsterhood, had saddled her with his despicable ways. She took it all in stride, amazing woman that she was. She deserved better. She deserved a man with passion for her, with appetites that would please her, a man who could give her babies, not a man who shunned her fine meals in favor of a cache of dried meat in his desk drawer and a swig of some alcohol with which to wash it down. She deserved better than a man who preferred the texture of a stiff vellum to her soft skin. She was a delightful social partner, conversationalist, and she must be starving, withering in this house where there were never social situations or conversations. There was no money, there was only Edgar, with his stinking clothing, his ill temper and his penchant to drink himself senseless over the images in his head that he could never articulate correctly.

And now she insisted he go out. He knew he needed to, but the page called to him as it always did.

"Get up, now," she said, and sent a mock frown from her reflection.

"I can't go," he said.

She sighed, then smiled at him with indulgence and affection, and began to dress.

~ ~ ~

Jan. 2. I have passed this day in a species of ecstasy that I find impossible to describe. My passion for solitude could scarcely have been more thoroughly gratified. I do not say satisfied; for I believe I should never be satiated with such delight as I have experienced to-day... The wind lulled about day-break, and by the afternoon the sea had gone down materially...Nothing to be seen, with the telescope even, but ocean and sky, with an occasional gull.

And there the words quit. The house was too quiet. The longed-for solitude too complete. The ecstasy of it too sublime.

When he awakened at his desk, the sun was sneaking around the sides of the pulled draperies, and Virginia had already left. He couldn't remember her errands, but thought he remembered her telling him that she'd be gone the whole day.

He was hardly ever alone in the house, and he was intrigued. He wanted to wander around, touching things he'd never touched before. He'd never even noticed many of her things of sentiment. The house was Virginia's domain, and he kept to himself and let her tend to all its needs. But now, with her gone—such a rare event—Edgar found his concentration completely broken by the pleasure of his own company.

Would nothing stop the distress? The images of his life upon the desolate shore—the ultimate solitude—would not leave him, yet he could not sit at that desk another minute. He craved brandy, but it was slowly poisoning him to death. He craved isolation, but when he had it, he couldn't take advantage of it.

Virginia should find herself a decent mate, he decided, and went back to his study where he and the blank page regarded each other for the rest of the day.

~ ~ ~

Jan. 3. A dead calm all day. Towards evening, the sea looked very much like glass. A few sea-weeds came in sight; but besides them absolutely nothing all day— not even the slightest speck of cloud…

Edgar felt a pounding in his head so severe he had to lift it. He'd been sleeping at his desk, as usual, head on his arms, and his arms were leaden and his head pounding.

He'd been heartbroken that the story he had begun with such promise was going nowhere. No plot, no characters—he was void. His quest for seclusion had finally found its way inside his skin and hollowed him out. He had no words but the unformed ones in his head, and they clawed at him like rats in the walls of his psyche.

Now they were not only scratching and hissing, but they had taken to pounding.

Pounding! He put his hands to his head to stop it.

No, the pounding was outside. Someone was at the door.

He cared not for intruders. He was within his light-house, his cylindrical home, the glass bottle of brandy that soothed him and kept the seas calm.

"Mister Poe?" More banging. "Mister Poe? Are you home, sir?"

Edgar dragged himself to his feet and stumbled to the kitchen door. The sunny room was about to blind him and when the pounding at the door stopped, it continued unabated in his head. "What is it?" he asked.

"Mister Poe, sir, my wife has sent me with a stew."

It took Edgar three tries to get the bolt thrown, but once he did, the next-door neighbor, a robust and ruddy Horace Wellington stood on the step, a cloth-covered dish in his hands.

"We haven't seen you about, Mr. Poe," Wellington said with a soft voice. "The wife is worried about you."

"I have no use for a stew—" Edgar began.

"But you do, sir, even I can see that," Wellington said, and pushed past Edgar as if he were but a wispy reed. He set the Dutch oven on the counter.

32

"No cooking has been done in here for a time," Wellington continued, and passed his hand across Virginia's spotless countertops. "Look here."

Poe rubbed the crust from his eyelids and, to humor his intruder, the more quickly to be rid of him, looked at the man's meaty palm.

"Dust, Mr. Poe," he said. "What are you living on? Here. Let me dish you up some of the missus's mutton here."

"No, thank you. I'm working," Edgar said, but the smell of the food made him salivate, and his stomach growled loudly.

"See there?" He got a dish from the cupboard and pulled out a chair for Edgar, who collapsed wearily. "Nice, nutritious victuals, Mr. Poe. Men like us, we need food like this."

Men like us, the neighbor said. *Men like us.*

Great spoonful were ladled into the dish, and steam wafted up. Edgar didn't know if he was going to faint or vomit. His stomach was greatly unsettled.

Instead, he coughed. The coughing was a bad fit—he supposed he picked it up with a chill—and took a while to complete. When it passed, it left him shaken and perspiring. He took some ragged breaths.

"Just a spoonful, if you please," Wellington said, and Edgar, so consumed with his breathing, was surprised to find him still there.

"Yes, all right," Edgar said, and took a spoonful of the broth. It smelled delicious and tasted even better. He helped himself to another spoonful.

"Maybe not too much," the man said. "You're looking a little tender."

Edgar looked up at him, spoon midway to his mouth. Tender. That had never been a word he'd use to describe himself. Tender. That wasn't right. He shook his head. The man was wrong. He was wrong about no cooking being done in the kitchen, too. Virginia had just gone for the day. Taken Hazel on errands, he supposed. But not tender. Never tender.

"Literary," he said.

"Pardon?"

"Not tender, literary."

"Yes, yes, of course," the man said, then motioned him to take another spoonful.

Edgar could see that the stupid man did not understand.

The stew warmed his belly, but his mind returned to images of tide and rock, of ships and beacons and solitude. Solitude. Precious insulation from well-meaning dolts such as Wellington and his fat wife.

He had another taste, thinking of the soundness of the structure he had created, the dark glass of the brandy bottle in which he lived—no, the light-house, *impenetrable by the sea with its solid iron-riveted wall. Fifty feet from the sea's high water mark, walls four feet thick, if one inch...*

"The missus and I would like you to take your meals with us in the evening, Mister Poe."

Edgar heard his words, but he would not let them penetrate. *Solid iron-riveted wall. Impenetrable.*

"Being a widower is no shame now."

Walls four feet thick if one inch.

"But dying yourself, all alone in this house, does sweet Mrs. Poe's memory no good, either."

Edgar squinted his eyes against the pain of the light, against the pain of the knowledge, against the pain of the intruder, against the pain, the anguish, the wretched torment of his solitude.

The basis on which the impenetrable structure rests seems to be nothing more than chalk, he thought, and the enormous, hot ball of emotion deep in his chest, deeper than the cough even, began to rise for the first time.

Sitting in his own kitchen, with a mere stranger next to him, Edgar's grief finally began to slosh about him, like an angry sea at high tide.

Anything

Marty drove around with the dead baby in his trunk for three days before he decided on a course of action. He knew he shouldn't be doing that; he needed to deal with the baby or else he needed to deal with Justanne; it was her baby. It got so he couldn't concentrate on anything at all. He just drove around and around, looking for a place to put it that wouldn't be disrespectful, but also wouldn't get him in trouble.

He knew the driving was dangerous—tempting fate. It was only a matter of time before he got rear-ended, or had to open his trunk for something, and then the vapors would escape and somebody would think it was his baby. Or that he had killed it.

He couldn't believe how tiny it was. Even wrapped up in a towel and then in a plastic grocery bag, it wasn't any bigger than a loaf of bread. On the second day, he put another towel around it and then a plastic bag from Wal-Mart and stashed it way in the back with the jumper cables where it wouldn't roll around. Something was going to leak out of that bag pretty soon, even if it was just odors. Police dogs could sniff out those fumes, he knew, because he'd seen it on some of those television shows, and soon his trunk would be full of them. Then they'd probably permeate the carpeting and stuff and he'd never be able to sell the stupid car.

He pounded on the steering wheel for the millionth time, raging at himself as he cruised past the mall.

He was so stupid to agree to take the baby from her to begin with. Now what used to be her problem had clearly become his problem.

He'd been asleep Sunday night when she called. The clock said 2:20 a.m., and that clock was always close enough to right to get him to work on time.

She was crying and hiccupping the way girls do when they get hysterical, and at first he thought she wanted him to take her to the hospital to have the baby, but eventually he figured out that she just wanted him to come over. She knew he would. He'd do anything for her, and she knew that. That was part of the problem.

He pulled on jeans and a t-shirt that didn't smell too bad and tiptoed up the basement steps of his parents' house. Still living at home was bad enough; waking them up or otherwise inconveniencing them might make them reconsider his fragile rental agreement. Once outside, he jogged to his car, an old black Toyota that barely ran, but was vehicle enough to get him back and forth to the convenience store where he worked.

As soon as he turned off the headlights in front of Justanne's house, she came out wearing a big coat and carrying a plastic bag. She opened the passenger side door, and Marty thought she was going to get in, but she just handed him the bag. "Here. Take this," she said and thrust it at him. Her face was all swollen and red and her hair was a wreck.

It was still warm. "Jesus God," Marty said.

"Just take it, please Marty, oh my god, please just take it away from me. I can't—I can't—" Then she turned and walked really fast back toward her house. When she got to the porch steps, she looked around at him. He just sat there, stunned. "Just hold it for me for a while," she said, then ran up the steps and went inside.

It was a yellow plastic bag from the grocery store. Inside was a towel, and Marty could see blood wicking through it. He set it on the passenger's seat and got out of there before anybody saw him, his heart beating so hard he saw red globes floating in front of his face.

He stopped at the Mini-Mart, tied the plastic bag handles together and then put it in the trunk. Then he went in for a cup of coffee, as if the situation warranted caffeine, and after that, he just started driving around.

Justanne was small, so most people would think it would be hard for her to hide a pregnancy, but she was sly. Everybody at school knew, but somehow she was able to keep it from her parents. Justanne was going steady with Rocky, but she confided in Marty. At least she used to.

One night she went over to Marty's after she'd had a fight with Rocky, and they had sex. It was his first time, but it wasn't hers, and when he found out later that she was pregnant, he hoped and prayed that it was his baby. He kept hoping and praying and waiting for some type of a sign from her, but as the months ticked down, hope faded. He still wished it was his, wished that Justanne would marry him and move into his parents' basement and be his family for at least a little while. But she never gave him any sign of encouragement, even though he tried to hang around and give her every opportunity.

One afternoon, Marty overheard his mother talking with a friend, and the friend said that all four of her sons were ten-month babies. That extended Marty's hope. But then once the baby ended up in his trunk, he no longer wished it was his. Now he hoped it was Rocky's.

He took another turn down State Street. If he knew for certain it was Rocky's, he'd throw it in a ditch. Or just put it in a garbage can. But as long as there was still a chance that it was his, he needed to do something else. Something besides just drive around.

He wondered if it was a boy or a girl. He knew he could go open the trunk and open the bag, unwrap it and look, but he was afraid to. He wondered what he and Justanne would have named it. He wondered if it would have grown up to look like Justanne, with her tiny blonde pixy looks, or him, tall and angular with thick black hair like his mom's.

That was the problem. He couldn't stop thinking long enough to make a decision, and until he could make a decision of some type, he was going to be driving around driving himself crazy and driving the vapors into the interior of his trunk.

~ ~ ~

After the third day of driving around, he knew he had to get back to work before Eddie stopped covering for him and he got fired. He went home, showered and changed clothes. He was nervous the whole time, needing to keep his keys within sight so his mom or his dad didn't decide to borrow his car and accidentally come upon the little surprise in the trunk. When he wiped the fog off the bathroom mirror, he thought he looked as hollow-faced and raggedy as he ever had. He was going to have to make a decision soon.

He parked where he could keep an eye on the car all day long and paced around the little store. Business was slow for a Thursday, and he thought a couple of times about lying on the floor behind the counter and sleeping for an hour, but every time he picked up the "closed" sign, somebody walked in looking for a gallon of milk or a pack of rolling papers, and he'd have to deal with them.

What he really wanted to do was grab one of those soft wussie SOB customers by the front of the shirt, bring his face close and whisper quietly, *"There's a dead baby in the trunk of my car. Do you think I have the time or patience to deal with you and your goddamned orange juice?"* But of course he never did. He worked his shift, went home and fell into bed, his keys held tightly in his fist. Just before he closed his eyes he prayed for an answer to his dilemma.

When he woke, he had it.

It was Justanne's baby, it was her problem, he needed to give it back to her.

He lay awake listening to the noises his parents made upstairs in the kitchen as they were getting ready to go to work, the soft murmur of their voices and the whir of the coffee grinder being familiar and comforting in this time of his insecurity and unsettledness. While he lay warm and cozy in his bed, looking at his favorite Lord of the Rings poster, he decided that he'd go to the high school, talk to Justanne, and if she wouldn't talk with him, he'd put the baby where somebody would find it. Maybe he'd leave it at the train station. Or in the mall. No, not the mall. Some place where they didn't have surveillance cameras. A church, maybe.

Anyway, first he needed to talk to Justanne. Face to face, not over the phone. He got up, went to work, and afterwards drove over to the high school.

As a dropout, Marty wasn't allowed on school property, not really, but he could sit in the circular drive with the buses and the moms waiting to pick up their kids. He stayed in the car, craning his neck for a glimpse of Justanne. He saw her skanky girlfriends, saw that they saw him, and watched as they all smirked and turned their backs to him. He didn't care. If Justanne was in school, she'd be with them. She wasn't.

He started up the Toyota and drove to her house, but Rocky's truck was parked in front, so he lost his nerve. He didn't know where to go, so he started driving around again, making himself nuts over the dead baby in the trunk.

Later, just before dusk, acid burning a hole in his gut, he decided he needed to get to Justanne, whether Rocky was there or not. He wasn't afraid of Rocky.

Yes, he was. Rocky was huge and muscular, and Marty was a dweeb. He knew it, but that was no reason to let Justanne saddle him with her crap.

He made his way to Justanne's house again, parked the Toyota behind Rocky's muscle truck and got out.

Rocky met him halfway up the drive. "Hey, loser," Rocky said. "What are you doing here?"

Marty tried to step around Rocky. "I came to see Justanne."

"She's not seeing you," Rocky said, took a step closer and bumped Marty with his chest.

We have something to talk about," Marty said.

"You don't got nothing to talk about, sow bug," Rocky said, "so get lost."

"Fuck you." Marty was amazed at himself, but not so amazed as when Rocky put his big meaty hands under Marty's arms, literally lifted him off his feet, and carried him a few steps down the driveway. Marty kicked at him, and Rocky let him go, let him drop a couple of inches, then kept shoving him back, shoving him back, so Marty could never quite get his balance. Rocky shoved him all the way back to the Toyota.

"Wait, wait, wait," Marty said. "Let me show you. Let me show you what I need to talk to Justanne about." He dodged Rocky, fished keys from his pocket and held them up for the big thug to see.

"Give me one good reason to give you another ten seconds of my life," Rocky said, but Marty could see that he was intrigued.

"You'll see." Marty opened the trunk and pointed to the baby in its towels and sacks, set in the middle of the loops of jumper cable. "There."

What?"

He pointed. When Rocky reached in deep to get the bag, Marty slammed the trunk lid hard down on his back, then grabbed the tire iron and whacked him hard across the back of the head. Rocky slumped, half in and half out, and it was a simple thing to lift his feet, tumble him into the trunk and close the lid.

It took about five seconds and nobody saw.

At least Marty was pretty sure nobody saw.

He got in the car and drove toward the MiniMart. He needed to put something substantial on top of all that coffee before it ate a hole in his belly.

But now he had two problems in his trunk and he had no idea what to do about either of them. Make that three problems. Rocky would be waking up soon and letting him out of the trunk wasn't going to be pretty. Marty really hadn't meant to do what he did. He had really meant to give Rocky the baby and be done with it, but his adrenaline was flowing, and his pride was wounded, and his manhood was being challenged, and when he saw his opportunity to give that big thick-necked asshole a smack, he couldn't help himself.

Justanne and her damned dead baby had driven him to it.

Perhaps he'd gone beyond the talking-to-Justanne option.

He needed to take Rocky and the baby out of town, far out of town, so he could dump them both and Rocky would have some time to think things over on his way back home. And he needed to gas up before Rocky came to and started banging on the inside of the trunk, calling attention to himself and his peculiar situation. Marty stopped at the MiniMart and filled the Toyota with gas. He got a hot dog when he went inside to pay and wolfed it down in three bites.

He drove out into the desert. It took him an hour—that would be good for Rocky's disposition—then he pulled off onto a side road that was nothing but dirt and weeds and followed it a long way into the dark from the main road.

Then he stopped, turned off the headlights and killed the engine. Rocky hadn't made a sound, and when Marty opened the trunk, he could see why.

A guy just can't catch a break these days, he thought to himself, as he hauled Rocky's dead carcass out of his trunk. Then he fetched the plastic Wal-Mart bag with the dead baby inside and set it on Rocky's dead chest, and placed Rocky's dead hand on top of it.

"There," he said out loud. "I'm fucking finished with this."

And with a sense of relief so enormous he could barely recognize himself within it, he got back into the Toyota and headed for Justanne's.

When she turned on the porch light and then opened the front door, Marty realized he didn't have anything prepared to say to her. He just wanted to look at her and let her know that he had taken care of her problem. He wanted her to know that she could count on him. He was adult enough, competent enough to deal with whatever life was going to throw at him, or whatever she was going to hand him.

Her face was scrubbed, her blonde hair was done up in a ponytail, and he noticed that she was out of the baggy shirts and back into her jeans. She had never looked prettier. "Hi, Marty," she said. She didn't invite him in. She looked over his shoulder and squinted at Rocky's truck, still parked in front of her house.

"Hi," he said. "I just came by to—" he tried to look around her to make sure nobody was listening— "to let you know that I took care of it."

"Took care of what?"

Marty rolled his eyes. "You know."

"No I don't."

"The *baby?*" he whispered.

"The baby? What baby?"

"*Your* baby, Justanne."

She stepped out onto the porch and closed the door behind her. "I don't know what you're talking about, Marty. What do you mean you took care of my baby?"

Marty started to get a little confused, but then he realized what her game was. She was going to play dumb and pretend none of it ever happened. It sure didn't increase his love for her. Maybe he was finally seeing her as she really was.

It didn't matter.

"Whatever, Justanne. I just want you to know I took care of it and you won't have to worry."

"You're not making any sense, Marty." She leaned against a column on her front porch and crossed her arms, a frown on her forehead.

"You know?" he said. "Last Sunday night?"

She looked confused for a moment, and then looked up at him wide-eyed. "The cat?" she said.

"Cat?"

"Yeah," she said. "Rocky brought over his stupid rottweiler and it killed my cat. You know Mystic? My big white cat? The dog chomped its head and killed it. I freaked out and couldn't deal with it and so I called you. What did you do with it?"

"Cat?" Marty was having trouble processing this new information. "What about the baby?"

"I had the baby Monday afternoon, a little girl, and we gave her up for adoption. She lives in Sacramento now."

Justanne uncrossed her arms and came across the porch to Marty, then gave him a long full-body hug, but not before he caught the wink of a small diamond on her left hand. "Adoption was the right thing to do," she said. "Rocky and I aren't ready for a family, but we're getting married after graduation." There was an awkward pause when Marty failed to return her embrace. "I hope you'll still be my best friend," she said.

Marty brought his arms up around her, holding her tight. He loved the feel of her small warm body pressed up against his. "I'd do anything for you, Justanne," he said, breathing in the scent of her. "Anything. You know that."

Chair

For some reason, as Claire trudged to work early on a Tuesday morning, instead of keeping her eyes straight ahead—or down on the cracked and pitched sidewalk to make sure she didn't trip—she looked left, down Second Street.

Second Street dead-ended at the Plant, and there, on the weedy lawn filled with dandelions, a man sat on a folding chair, his face held up to the early morning sun.

Scandalized, Claire pulled her sweater tight around her bony ribcage and hurried on to work. "Looney," she muttered.

The next day, Claire didn't need to look, and she knew she shouldn't have, but her eyes betrayed her as she hustled across Second Street, and she chanced a glance.

He was there, and this time there was a second chair, an *empty* chair, next to him.

This looked like an invitation, and Claire started to walk quickly toward her job in the zipper factory, where she had worked for decades, and knew everything about her job there was to know. She was comfortable in her little apartment, she was comfortable doing her job, and except for the days when the weather made it dangerous to walk the six blocks to work, her routine suited her.

But now this man and his apparent invitation bothered her, so much that she thought about him at work and wondered why he would sit so close to the Plant with its ominous blank gray concrete walls, and before she knew it, she cut a zipper one centimeter too short. The eye in the ceiling saw it immediately and dispatched a drone to escort her upstairs.

"Your mind is not on your work, Claire," the supervisor said.

Claire kept her eyes on the toes of her shoes. She didn't like looking at the supervisor. For one thing, his facial features were disproportionate in a very unattractive way, and he continually twirled a rubber band around his fingers which made her nervous, and for another thing, she didn't want him to think she was insubordinate.

"I'm sorry, sir," she said. "It won't happen again."

"It's not just one zipper, Claire," the supervisor said.

She wished he wouldn't say her name. She didn't want the sound of her name to come from his ugly mouth.

"We don't want it to become a trend. We don't want this to be the first of a whole series of accidents and mishaps, do we?"

"No, sir," Claire said.

"Is something bothering you? It's my job, you know, to help people who have troubles. We don't want people with troubles working here at Worldwide Zipper."

"No, sir, no troubles. I just lost my concentration for a moment."

"A moment is all it takes, Claire," he said, only this time he put some kind of a weird drawn-out accent on her name, to make it sound like he was mocking her. She feared she would hate her name from this moment on.

"It won't happen again."

"Back to work!" he commanded. The door opened, and the drone appeared at her side.

Chagrined, Claire returned to her workstation and made certain she measured correctly for the rest of the day.

The next day, she woke up to a light rain, so she dressed warmly and carried her compact black umbrella, but once again, she could not keep her eyes to herself, and as she glanced over, the man was sitting next to the Plant, a huge colorful umbrella covering both him and the empty chair next to him.

He smiled at her. She could see his teeth, even two blocks away, a sure sign of lunacy. Heat flushed through Claire's face, and she hurried on to her job, vowing to take a different route home and find a different way to work the next day that didn't provide such uncomfortable temptations as to look at the crazy man sitting in the weedy lot.

But it wasn't the man who troubled her all day at work, it was the empty chair, the quiet, peaceful invitation to join him sitting there in the weeds, smiling, next to the wall of the Plant. What could he want with her? What could he be thinking and doing over there all by himself, with a chair that just anyone could come along sit down in?

By the end of her workday, Clair had begun to worry that someone else would be sitting in that chair the next morning.

She got up early, hesitation in every action, but worry that someone else would be sitting in her chair gave her purpose. Filled with worry and anxiety, she left her apartment and strode toward Second Street.

He was there, sitting in the sunshine.

He waved at her.

She put her head down and walked toward him, down the unfamiliar sidewalk, across the street and didn't even hesitate when she stepped onto the grass of the weedy lot. She walked directly to the empty chair and sat down.

"Hi," the man said.

Clair didn't exactly feel the need to communicate with him, but she didn't want to be rude. "Hi," she answered.

They sat in silence for a good four minutes before she got up. She didn't want to leave his side, didn't want to leave the weeds, didn't want to leave the extraordinarily comfortable chair, even though it was just a little green folding chair, but to stay and lose her job was inconceivable, so she got up and hurried off to work.

The next day she got up earlier and sat in his chair a couple of minutes longer.

The next day she got up even earlier and sat in his chair even longer.

And the next day was her day of rest. She got up and got dressed as usual and walked toward the weedy lot and the man in the chair.

He was there, as usual, and this time she had no reason to hurry away. A calming peace came over her as she sat next to him, just sitting quietly in the early morning sunshine.

"Companionship," he said. His voice had a melodic quality she had never heard before, and she had to consciously keep herself from looking at him in open-mouthed amazement. She wanted to stare at him, to drink in every detail of his face, but she dared not even look at him.

Companionship. She had heard that word before but had never really understood the concept until this very moment. What a great idea. She loved companionship.

The sun rose high in the sky and still they sat, not talking. Claire began to think of her future, of possibilities she had never considered before. She wanted to take up a pencil and draw things. She wanted to draw his picture and wondered if she even had a pencil or paper in her apartment. In a strange way, she couldn't quite remember what her apartment looked like, nor what she did at her job. Not while she was sitting next to this intriguing man, not while she was sitting in the shadow of the Plant.

"It's leaking," the man said, when Claire stood up to leave because she was getting cold in the shadow of the wall.

She looked at him for the first time, and his face was gloriously soft and genuine. He smiled with even, strong teeth and crinkles at the corners of his kind eyes. "Leaking?"

He nodded. "The Plant is leaking. My son discovered it."

"Your son?"

He nodded, smiled a sad smile, turned inward, and rocked back and forth a little bit.

Claire wrapped her sweater around herself and walked away through the wet weeds.

"Come back tomorrow," he called after her.

Even though she knew the word, suddenly the idea of tomorrow was a fresh concept. A new feeling grew in her chest, and she looked forward, maybe for the first time ever, to tomorrow.

The next day, the man stood up when she approached and began talking even before she sat down in the chair. He spoke with some urgency, as if he had to tell her everything in the ten minutes she had before she had to leave for work.

"My son saw the carts in the night from his bedroom window. They come out of little doors on the other side of the Plant, and they go to certain houses in the city. We thought the Plant was closed or deserted or something, but it isn't. He found out that the houses where the carts went to were houses with new babies, and where people were dying."

That seemed so incredibly odd to Claire that it didn't even seem possible. Was her companion just a lunatic after all?

"We think they deliver hope," he said.

"Hope?" Claire didn't even know what that was.

The man sighed. "It's all in here," he cocked his head toward the Plant. "It's all in here, and now it's leaking. That's why I sit here, because it feels so good. That's why *you're* here."

He *was* crazy! Claire got up and ran. She ran all the way to the zipper factory and arrived out of breath. Her coworkers stepped away from her as if she had something contagious. Nobody ever ran in the city. There was nothing to run to, nothing to run from.

But Claire had found something so confusing that she ran from it, and now, suddenly, she wanted to run back to it.

She didn't know what she thought, except that she needed to keep her mind on her job and she needed to go back to the Plant wall and sit in the weeds with the man again tomorrow.

But the next morning, he wasn't there.

Claire went to the empty area where his chairs used to be; she could still see the marks on the ground where their feet had mashed the weeds into the soggy soil. She stood in the space where her chair—at least she had come to view it as her chair—had sat, and she waited for him.

She closed her eyes and let the sun warm her face. She felt the hope emanating from the concrete walls of the Plant behind her, and her mind opened to a million possibilities. She never had to go back to the zipper factory, never had to face the ugly supervisor again. She could leave the city. She could just sit here and wait for the man to come back, and then go to live with him and his son and they could have hope together. They could sit right here in the sun together every day and bring another chair and another and another and invite people to join them and find this same kind of newness. She could live in a little tent, right here next to the Plant and soak up all that was emanating from it.

Life was full of possibilities, as long as she was here, as long as she was close to the wall.

She never wanted to leave.

"Claire!" Startled, she looked up, and the supervisor stood in the middle of the street. "Come along, or you'll be late for work."

Claire looked down at her shoes so she wouldn't have to look at his face. She didn't want to go to work. She wanted to stand right here. She wanted to run back to her little apartment and get a chair—two chairs—and drag them right back here to this spot, so that when the man came back, he'd have a place to sit and companion.

"Claire?"

"It's leaking," she said, and in a burst of compassion for the ugly supervisor who made her life so gray, she invited him to join her. "Come here and feel it."

"It's toxic waste," he said. "You'll go mad."

"No," she said, wondering how it could be that she was talking to her supervisor in this manner, "it's leaking hope."

"I'll report you if you get contaminated," he said. "I had to report the man who has been sitting here all that time."

"Why?" she asked. "Why would you do that?"

"Someone had to," the supervisor said. "Come along now."

Claire stood quietly for a long moment, considering her options, then one step at a time, she walked toward him through the wet weeds.

"You will have to sit all day with wet feet," he said.

"Yes," she said, and then remembered.

"Didn't your wife just have a baby?" she asked.

"Yes. Two weeks ago."

So he had hope. He got a glass of it, or a package of it, or a dose of it, or something, just recently. He had it at home; he didn't have to sit in the weeds next to the concrete wall in order to feel it.

"How did the hope get inside the Plant?" she asked him as they walked toward the factory.

"The Plant is abandoned," he said. "There's nothing inside the building."

Claire didn't believe him, but the further she got from it, the less it mattered.

"What happens when you report someone?" she asked.

47

The supervisor opened the employee door to the Worldwide Zipper Factory. "That's not our concern," he said. "We're here to make zippers and make them correctly." He paused and looked at her. "I hope you don't go back there again. Nothing good will come of it."

There it was again, that word, hope.

She didn't answer him, but went straight to her workstation and cut zippers to their perfect length all day long, and when she went home, she looked at the only chair in her apartment and thought about how it would look next to the Plant.

Pathetic, she decided. She had no second chair; she had no colorful umbrella. She could not companion.

In the morning, she left at the usual time for work. As she crossed Second Street, she glanced down, but nothing was there but the weedy lot and the gray wall of the Plant.

The supervisor was probably right, she thought. Toxic waste. Nothing good could come of it.

Charlie's Grave

The note said simply, *Charlie died and your dad had a stroke burying him. Come home.* Laura assumed that the Reverend Mathews wrote the note and addressed the envelope, per her mother's request. It wasn't her mother's handwriting; her mother had no handwriting. And her mother would insist that the reverend not embellish the message at all, either. There were no embellishments, not even a signature. There were certainly no sentiments.

Laura canceled her appointments for the next three days and had her secretary book a flight and a rental car.

Finally, it was time to go home.

In a way, she was sad she had waited so long that she wouldn't be seeing her dad. But then, she never expected to see either of her parents again. She never wanted to. And she didn't want to now, but she couldn't ignore this summons.

She never expected that her mother would need her.

She only hoped her mother didn't need her too much. Laura had a busy, full life, and while she wasn't proud of the thoughts she had about her illiterate, dirt-poor parents and their lifestyle, she wasn't about to compromise her hard-won financial independence and freedom from that sticky-mud rural mountain rootball.

Every Christmas, Laura tucked a couple of hundred-dollar bills into her Christmas card to them, and she assumed the money was received, though it was never acknowledged. They had had no other communication since Laura moved away to go to college on a merit scholarship over twenty years before. Her books were her life. She got straight A's all the way through college, cementing her grants and loans and scholarships, studying summers and during term breaks. She worked part time in various medical laboratories, gaining important research experience as well as extra credit. She taught basic biology while getting her graduate degree, and once firmly ensconced as a research assistant in one of the larger pharmaceutical companies, wrote her dissertation and acquired her Ph.D.

Nice looking, soft spoken, hard driven and dedicated, she turned out to be Mymet Laboratory's biggest gun in soliciting research grants.

Her dirt farm heritage was a nasty little secret that she didn't want anyone to discover. She hated owning that attitude, but over the years, it had become a habit.

At first, she was too busy to go home. School and work tied her nose to the grindstone, and she couldn't get away, couldn't afford to get away to go back.

Then she was too proud to return home. She had nice clothes. She could read and write. She studied the classics in literature classes. She mapped DNA genomes. She was a whiz at math and chemistry. She didn't know what she would talk about with her parents. She didn't want to see them through educated eyes.

Then she was too political to go back. Her high-paid future at Mymet was predicated on her gracious, well-timed ability to extract big bucks from those government agencies that held the grants. She also spoke at stockholder meetings, where she impressed not only the board of directors, but those who held large blocks of preferred Mymet stock. Most of those people were old-money, conservative, squeaky clean people and they wanted those they associated with to have the same pristine background. Or at least the illusion of it. Laura worked hard to feel at home in those circles.

Then, as time and experience funneled wisdom into her head, almost against her will, she was too ashamed of herself to swallow her pride and come back home to the family she had deserted so many years ago.

And now Charlie was dead, her daddy was too, like as not, and her mama needed her. "Time to grow up, Laura," she told herself. "You'll turn forty this year. It's time to reconcile."

She knew her mama would die someday, and her daddy too, but Charlie? Charlie was never supposed to die.

On the plane, Laura made a fearless, realistic appraisal of her life. She was professionally successful and personally a disaster. She had no mate; she rarely even dated. She owned a nice, professionally-decorated apartment that had no soul. She had two good women friends, but distance was necessitated by her fictional history. They were professional colleagues before they were friends, and once she had told them the fabricated story of her middle-class upbringing, it had to add up on all fronts.

Laura kept a tight rein on her life. So tight it pinched. It choked her. Laura was afraid that if she eased up in any area—acquiring a boyfriend, getting intimate with girltalk, going on a wild spree of any kind, be it a rummy vacation in the Bahamas or a new hairdo or a trendy wardrobe or a whimsical redecoration of her bedroom—that she would lose the steel bands that kept the staves of her carefully designed and constructed persona together.

If those bands ever loosened, backwoods dirtwater would leak out of her, pool on her thick-pile beige carpeting and she'd leave a barefoot, pigshit stench wherever she went.

She'd worked too hard to pull herself out of that sty; she refused to be sucked back into it.

But acknowledging her roots didn't mean having to move back into the dirt floor shack, now, did it?

Her only pair of jeans—expensive designer jeans—were in the weekender valise in the overhead compartment. She had bought a pair of tennis shoes and a couple of light cotton tops she could throw away when this trip was over. And she had packed a black dress, anticipating her daddy's funeral. She'd see to her mama, and then she'd go back to her high-rise apartment, and back to her enviable life.

Who knew what she would actually find, once she actually got back to West Virginia? Older versions of the same kids she went to school with, she imagined. Working at the dime store and slinging hash at Tiddly's just like their parents did. They'd each have too many sickly kids with ringworm and lice, and they'd live in old run-down trailers with rusted car carcasses in the front yards, leggy weeds growing up through their transmissions and out from under their bent up hoods.

Laura felt sick to her stomach just thinking about it. She opened the in-flight magazine and looked at the upcoming year in fashion.

~ ~ ~

Enid Bridges heard from Dannie Brooks that her daughter had booked a room for three nights in her little bed and breakfast in town. Enid couldn't quite imagine that Dannie had the guts to rent out her son's old room, add a stack of flapjacks and call it a Bed and Breakfast, although she guessed that's exactly what Dannie offered. A bed. And breakfast. Dannie's old house was right next to the post office, so it was in a central location, not way out Highway 38, like Enid and Whip's place.

But Dannie wasted no time driving her old Ford on out to tell Enid that Laura was coming, and for that, Enid was grateful, if a bit shamed that the neighbors knew about it before she did. And they knew that Laura wouldn't stay in her own room in her own house. And now, on the morning of the day Laura was supposed to arrive, Enid looked around and didn't know what to do to prepare for her daughter's arrival.

The house was clean, Whip was bathed and fed, and now slept peacefully on the sofa, the television giving him comfortable background noise. She'd changed the sheets on the bed Laura wasn't going to use and put out fresh towels. A chicken stewed on the stove, and Enid had baked a cake the night before.

The chickens took care of their ownselves nowdays, and after Charlie died, Enid went down to the police station and asked Mort if he'd come take the two horses and four young beefs to the auction for her. Mort and his son came by the following Saturday morning, and left behind an empty barn and a simpler, emptier life for Enid.

The chores were done, the house was ready, there was nothing for her to do now, but wait.

She paced the scrubbed kitchen floor one more time, then looked in on her husband. When he was sleeping, he looked like a normal man. It was only when he was awake, and trying to talk, or laugh, or eat, or be normal that she could see the sag to the left side of his face. He tried to be Whip, he tried real hard, but a chunk of him was gone. He left a big part of him up on the knoll, Enid figured.

There was nothing sadder than to see the mortality of one's mate. She'd always hoped she'd die first, so as to never have to face life without Whip, but over the years she had grown strong, strong enough to help him through this, strong enough to see the end of their days, strong enough to hope that he died first.

She'd become strong enough to endure being abandoned by their only child. Strong enough to insist that Laura come home. And Laura was coming. Today.

Whip needed to see Laura if only for the last time before he died. And

Laura needed to see her daddy. There wasn't anything Enid could do to change Laura's feelings about her family, though she would if she could. Laura had always been a high-spirited girl. And smarter by far than her parents by the time she was old enough for school. By the time she was in high school, she was spending all night, it seemed, at the little library, and she'd bring those big books home and try to talk about them at the dinner table.

Enid tried, God knows she tried to talk to her girl, but the things Laura said confounded her and made as much sense as Chinese. Whip used to get mad and throw down his napkin, but Enid knew it wasn't Laura's fault—she was cursed with a big brain, and a yearning for knowledge that came from somewhere outside their family traits. Enid was proud of her, but afraid that all that book studying would come to no good when it came time to find a husband, raise a family and cook the daily meat and potatoes. All that knowledge just puts restlessness in the soul. Or so she believed.

But she really didn't know. For all she knew, Laura had married well and had a passel of her own kids.

Except that Enid knew her daughter's heart well enough—or hoped she did—that if Laura had children, she'd want them to meet their grandparents, even if the only book those grandparents owned was the one that held the bedroom door from slamming.

No, Enid was certain that Laura had never married, had never had a child. Enid felt it was in some way her fault that Laura was born so smart that she'd put her priorities all in the wrong order. It was as if Enid and Whip were supposed to have seven or eight kids, but when the time came, and they were only given the one, that one, that poor Laura, was cursed with the smarts of all seven or eight.

And that made her a misfit. The life of a misfit was never an easy one. Enid prayed every day that with all those smarts of Laura's, she'd figure out a way to fit in. Well, they'd see, wouldn't they? Laura was coming home. Today. Enid fingered the worn lace on the edge of her fresh apron and tried not to worry.

~ ~ ~

Laura pulled into the driveway, scattering chickens. It was exactly the same. The driveway, the barn, the house, everything. Everything was exactly the same. She couldn't believe it.

Then a short, white-haired woman came out the kitchen door, and Laura barely recognized her mother. But the way Enid held on to the screen door so it wouldn't slam, and the way she took tentative steps down the shaky porch stairs, then held her hands clasped in front of her was as familiar and recognizable as the way out to this old farmhouse. Her fingers tugged on a threadbare apron that Laura remembered—an apron that should have been a dust rag twenty years ago.

She got out of the car and the silence of the country stunned her for a moment. She had to consciously take a breath. It, too, was familiar, as if it had been bred into her genes, and she'd been fooling herself by living in the city all these years.

"Hi, Mama," she said simply, and walked around the back of the car to hug her tiny mother. Enid even smelled the same. Ivory soap and baby powder.

"It's good to have you home," Enid said. "I know your father will be happy to see you."

"Daddy? I thought—"

"It won't be long now," Enid said. "Come see him while you still can."

Laura walked up those same split porch steps, through that same loose screen door and into that same, scrubbed kitchen. It was almost exactly the same—perhaps a little shabbier. The worn black spot in the middle of the kitchen sink had grown, the kitchen curtains were a little thinner from the sun and the regular washings, the wallpaper a little more faded. The linoleum had worn in a path right down to the black mastic. But the Blue Delphi plates were still on the walls and her high school graduation picture was still taped to the ancient refrigerator door.

"Whip?" Enid said and walked through the kitchen into the living room.

Laura heard her mother click off the television. She didn't want to go in there, but she had to, she knew she had to.

"Guess who's come to see you, honey? Can you sit up?"

Laura heard groaning and a couple of low syllables as she imagined her mother readied her father for company. "Come on in," Enid called.

Laura stepped around the corner into her childhood. The living room was exactly the same. Even the same old black and white television.

But her father wasn't. Thin and with few strands of white hair left, he sat propped up in the corner of the couch, surrounded by pillows. His pencil legs were covered by a crocheted Afghan, and the scarred, working-man fingers of one hand played the piano in midair.

"Hi, Daddy," Laura said, and his eyes brightened as he recognized her, but his mouth stayed still. She sat on the sofa next to him, and a tear tripped off of his lower lid and skidded down his old cheek that was lined from the sun and dotted with dark brown spots.

"F-f-f-goddamn!" he said.

Enid laughed with fondness at him, while Laura looked at him in confusion. "He has a hard time talking," she said, "but he can still cuss."

Laura kissed his cheek, and though his father fragrance had turned to an old-man odor, she could still detect sunshine and fertilizer, hay and cow manure. Fresh farm smells. She took his restless hand in hers and kissed it, then held it still in her lap. There were no words for her emotion. There wasn't even any definition to her emotion. She was overwhelmed, and she didn't know what it was that overwhelmed her.

"Lemonade?" Enid asked.

"F-f-f-goddamn!" Whip said, another tear following the first down into a crease in his cheek, and he squeezed Laura's hand. She wished he'd squeeze it hard enough to squeeze a tear out of her eye. She felt full to bursting.

Enid brought three glasses of lemonade into the living room and opened the curtains to let in the late afternoon sun. "So," she said. "Dandy new car."

"It's a rental," Laura said.

"I always liked a red car."

Laura watched as her mother helped her father sip some lemonade, more of it going down his chin than in his mouth. She laughed, teasing him with great affection as he groaned his frustration. She wiped his face, kissed his cheek, and then sat down again in a straight-backed chair on the other side of the coffee table.

The coffee table had the same empty nut dishes that had been there when Laura was a kid, each perched daintily on its own hand-crocheted doily.

"Married?" Enid asked.

"No, Mama," Laura said, indignation rising. "Don't you think I'd let you know if I got married or had any kids?"

"Don't know," Enid said. "I'd hope so, though. Too late now, don't you think?"

Laura looked across the table at the woman who had given birth to her but who was now a stranger and Laura was amazed at her lack of propriety. That topic of discussion was way too personal. And yet. And yet, this was her mother.

She felt a familiar attitude coming on. She stepped into this house and she became a child again.

Well, she wasn't a child, and she didn't have to put up with being made to feel like one.

Laura felt her blood pressure rise.

Relax, she told herself. *Just relax.*

"Suppose so," she said, telling herself that she could do this, she could endure this for a couple of days and then she could go home again, back to Minnesota, back to where she was comfortable, back to where she was a competent adult, back to where she knew who she was and what she was about. This would be but a very short period of time. She'd been uncomfortable before; she could put up with it.

Whip pulled his hand from Laura's and began waving it around and making sounds with a mouth that didn't work and a tongue that lay flat.

"He wants to know how long you're staying," Enid translated.

"I'm going home Thursday," Laura said. "I have to leave here about noon."

Whip looked at Enid.

"Today's Tuesday," she said to him.

He nodded, put his hand back into his daughter's, then said something else that sounded like wailing to Laura.

"No, honey," Enid said. "She's staying down at Dannie's."

A pang of guilt grabbed Laura. "I could stay here," she said. "I just didn't want to be any trouble," she said.

"No trouble," Enid said. "Wherever you're comfortable."

Whip pulled his hand away from Laura's again, and with a finger, stabbed the sofa between them. She didn't need any translation.

"Okay, Daddy," she said. "I'll stay here."

He nodded again, then looked at Enid.

"He's ready for dinner, Laura," she said. "Will you help me in the kitchen?"

～ ～ ～

The television provided background noise, the stew pot bubbled with delicious smells, as Laura set places for two at the kitchen table, and for one on the coffee table, per her mother's instructions. Enid mixed up dough for dumplings and they worked around each other in silence. If Laura closed her eyes, she could be a child again, her father due home for dinner from the fields, Charlie in the living room watching cartoons, Laura reluctantly setting the table when she'd rather be upstairs immersing herself in either her schoolwork or a novel that transported her far, far away from West Virginia.

She still wanted to be transported far, far away.

The air here smelled the same. It had that same, poor, illiterate stink to it that she had always hated. That hadn't changed. That would never change.

"Here," Enid said, handing Laura a bowl of chicken and dumplings. "Go help your daddy, while I ice this here cake."

Laura didn't like being ordered around, but she was glad for something to do, and it wouldn't be a bad thing to help her father eat.

But feeding him was a terribly frustrating process.

By the time she realized that the kitchen towel her mother handed her along with the bowl of soup was to put around his neck, she had dribbled chicken broth all down the front of his shirt. His swallowing was impaired, and she had to cut the chicken up into pieces so small it was almost as if she was chewing it for him, and every other mouthful he'd choke and cough and she would begin to panic.

"I'm sorry, Daddy," she said, close to tears. "I'm not very good at this."

"Me, neither," he said as clearly as if his language apparatus worked perfectly. What he did was make an incomprehensible sound, but Laura understood. She smiled, the tears overflowing her lower lids this time, and gave him a hug.

"F-f-f-goddamn!" he said, and they both laughed, or as close to it as they could come.

By the time he gave up, she had fed him maybe half a bowl of soup, and spilled another third of it down the front of him. She kissed his temple and took everything back into the kitchen.

"He eat?" Enid was dishing up their bowls.

"About half."

"That's good. His appetite has been waning."

"I kind of made a mess."

"It takes practice. I'll clean him up."

Laura put ice water in their two glasses, then carried the steaming bowls to the table. Maybe it was a good thing she'd never married, she thought. She'd never be able to take care of somebody like this. Never. Her mother fed him three, maybe four times a day, helped him bathe, shave, go to the bathroom, dress, sleep, oh god, no way. No way.

"We thank you for the money you send every Christmas," Enid said.

Laura smiled.

"You must be doing good up there in Minnesota."

"It's a good job. It's a challenge, and a lot of fun. Next month I go to Washington to testify before Congress."

"No." Enid stopped doing what she was doing, turned and looked at her daughter with admiration all over her face. "Congress? The real Congress? In Washington, D.C.?"

"Yeah. It's about, you know, drugs. We want our new drugs approved by the FDA, because we could help people who need them, but the government makes us jump through too many hoops."

"What kind of drugs?"

"Well, we've developed a pill that can cure a yeast infection with only one dose. We think it should be available over the counter."

"You got anything that could help your daddy?"

Laura looked down at her plate. "No, Mama. Has he seen a doctor? Did you take him to the hospital? He should be on some blood thinners or something."

"No, no hospital. They'll just try to make him live longer, and he don't want to, not like this."

"Stroke victims sometimes recover lots of their former faculties. If he had some therapy..."

Enid just shook her head.

"Nobody thought Charlie'd ever speak, either," Laura said. "Or dress himself. But he did,"

"Charlie was a little boy. God made children like little rubber balls. Your daddy, his bounce is gone." Enid smiled. "He spent it right, and he used it all up."

She was right, Laura knew. It was so odd to hear her mother talking of her husband's death without putting up a fight, though. She accepted it as if... as if... as if death were a part of life. Which it was, and Laura ought to know that by now.

~ ~ ~

Her old bedroom looked like a guest room, and Laura even had conflicting feelings about that. On one hand, she hoped they had preserved her childhood in there, and on the other hand, she hoped they hadn't clung to her like that. And now that she saw they hadn't, she kind of wished they had. The furniture was the same, but the walls were newly white and the quilt and curtains were fresh. Everything of her childhood was gone, and the room was cool and as sterile as a room with hand sewn quilts could be. They'd moved on. Did she think she had so much power over them that they would pine for her year after year for twenty years?

Laura snuggled down in the cool sheets with the warm quilt over her and listened for Charlie in the next room. But this wasn't her room anymore, she wasn't in high school anymore, and Charlie didn't sleep next door anymore.

"One day down," she said to herself, punched the pillow, took a deep breath of the familiar scent of her old room and reached for sleep.

~ ~ ~

Enid got her husband cleaned up, into his pajamas, and settled down on the sofa for the night. He lived on the sofa now and would for the rest of his days.

She turned off the television and sat with him for a while, holding his hand, running her thumb back and forth across his forehead.

Laura will want to go see Charlie's grave tomorrow. Maybe she'll drive that fancy red car into town and see some of her old friends, too.

"She's a beautiful girl," she said softly to Whip. "Smart and successful." A certain sadness mixed with the pride she felt. She was so happy to have raised an independent girl, an educated girl, who escaped the beatings of a drunken husband and the life of raising a dozen shoeless kids—the life so many of her classmates had fallen into.

But there seemed to be a certain soullessness to Laura's life instead. No husband to beat her, but yet no husband at all. Enid looked with fondness at Whip, who began to twitch in the early stages of falling asleep. What would her life have been about if it hadn't been about Whip? And no children for Laura, either. What would Enid have to be proud about if it wasn't for Laura? And Charlie, too, she supposed, though he wasn't hers by birth, he might as well have been. And though he grew to be a man, and they treated him like a man, he was always and forever a child.

Oh God, she missed Charlie more than she thought was possible. She didn't think she'd even miss Whip as much when he passed on.

Charlie had come to them so young, maybe six or seven, nobody really knew. He'd been dropped off or left behind or something at Tiddly's. Told the waitress his name was Charlie, but that's pretty much all he said before the accident over at the Sinclair station. He'd been sleeping in the pile of old catalogs in the back, begging for food with those blue eyes of his and that quick smile. The men took to feeding him like any stray, and he hung around, watching the men wrench on those engines. One afternoon, Charlie was sitting on a stack of tires, watching the men, when an air hose busted loose from the compressor, snicked around and the brass end of it crushed a hole in the boy's skull.

Whip was there filling up the gas cans for his tractor when it happened, and he grabbed the boy and brought him home.

Enid boiled up some darning needles, some sharps and a spool of thread, and with Charlie's head in her lap and his blood soaking through towels, she pulled up the pieces of bone by their edges until they pretty closely matched the curvature of his head. Then she sewed up the tear in his scalp with her sewing kit, wrapped the boy's head and put him to bed in the spare room next to Laura's.

The next day he woke, and he could eat, but his eyes were vacant. It was a good month before life returned to those eyes. It was two years before language came to the boy, and maturity, never. But he grew big and strong and loyal and hard working. He helped Whip with all the chores and acted like a little brother to Laura, and never failed to kiss Enid's cheek when he left for chores after breakfast or when he came home for dinner. Never missed. Never forgot.

Oh, she missed those kisses.

Laura was just a baby when Charlie came to them, and she mentally passed him up before she was three. But she seemed to understand that he was damaged, and while she never doted on him, she was never mean to him, either. She just accepted him as being who he was, an older brother, kind of, who was always younger.

In the dark hours of the night, when sleep eluded her, Enid wondered if Laura had forsaken the family because too much of her time was spent with Charlie. He was needier, so he got more attention. Would Laura be softer and have a bigger heart and a more normal life today if she had been raised with normal brothers and sisters? Or if she had been an only child?

What if Laura knew that Charlie cried for six months after she left? What if Enid told her that every Christmas when a beautiful card full of money came from the postman, Charlie would grab the card and have Enid tell him stories about Laura and the angels, for surely she lived with angels in Minnesota, or she wouldn't send pictures of them every year. Then the card would disappear into his room.

If Laura only knew how much Charlie missed her. Would that make a difference to her?

Or would telling her just make her feel bad? What good would it do now?

"I did the best I could with what I had and what I knew at the time," she said softly to Whip, whose eyes fluttered open for a moment, then closed again. "I always tried to do right," she said, feeling the softness of Charlie's lips on her cheek, the freshness of his shave in the mornings, the buzz of his heavy reddish beard stubble in the afternoons. She thought of her beautiful daughter, asleep upstairs, and wondered when she last got a kiss on the cheek from Laura.

So different, Enid thought.

I did the best I could at the time, she thought. And I'll do the best I can tomorrow, too.

She kissed her husband's forehead, tucked the Afghan up around his neck, turned off the light and went into her bedroom, leaving the door open in case he needed her in the night.

~ ~ ~

Tiddly's was exactly the same, except the faux-leather booths were now black instead of red. Laura wasn't really hungry, not after that enormous breakfast her mother made, but she wanted to cruise through town, and Tiddly's was the center of the social whirl.

First she settled up with Dannie Brooks—she hadn't cancelled her reservation, so she paid anyway, despite Dannie's protests. Dannie fussed over her like a visiting diplomat, which made Laura uneasy, but she exited Dannie's foyer as quickly and as gracefully as good manners would allow. Dannie walked her out to the car, admired the rented Ford, then said, "Sorry about your Daddy, Laura." Then before Laura could respond, Dannie added, "and Charlie, of course."

There. Somebody had finally said his name. Tears bloomed in Laura's eyes, and she accepted Dannie's hug, squeaked out a "thank you," got in her car, and blew her nose.

Enid hadn't said anything about Charlie. Laura began to wonder how he died. Why he died. He was only, what, forty-six? He was supposed to be there to take care of the folks, to be their son, their grandson, their great-grandson, to see them through the rest of their lives.

He was supposed to be there, absent Laura. He was to be the one to assuage her guilt.

What happened?

She repaired her makeup and drove the two blocks to the cafe. When she walked in, she remembered a few good times, when she felt a part of a crowd, and she remembered the bad times, when she felt ostracized by everybody.

Most specifically, she remembered giving Randall Cosgrove his ring back in that corner booth. She'd cried as she slowly unwound the angora yarn from it, making him as uncomfortable as she could, for as long as she could, and the next day that same ring was on a chain around Cynthia Newcomb's neck.

Laura sat at the counter and ordered coffee, and it wasn't until it was served that she recognized the waitress. Lisa Mae Wolff.

Lisa Mae recognized her at the same instant, squealed and ran around the counter for a hug, then called into the back that she was taking a break. A younger, high school age girl came out to take her place. The café wasn't busy, so she set herself to refilling sugar dispensers.

Laura and Lisa Mae slid into a booth, where Lisa Mae lit up a cigarette and moaned about her feet, then they settled right down to gossiping. Lisa Mae still wore her hair bleached yellow and ratted high up on her head. Her lipstick and nail polish were as pink as the apron she wore over a white blouse and jeans. They had never been very good friends in high school, but all that class distinction seemed to melt away in the perspective of life in their forties. They talked and laughed about all their old classmates, most of whom lived an unenviable life.

"But look at you!" Lisa Mae said with admiration in her eyes. "We always knew you were too smart to stick around here. You escaped this place, and it was a good thing you did. You're the only one who did. Some got as far as Wheeling, but that's not far enough. Most settled right here, or down yonder."

Laura knew that "down yonder" meant the hollow with the tin shacks and old rundown travel trailers. Alcoholism, disease, incest and murder weren't uncommon down there. Living down yonder was a horrible life sentence, and Laura didn't know how people ended up there, knowing about it the way everybody did, but there were never many vacancies there.

"How many kids you got?" Lisa Mae asked.

"No kids," Laura said. "I never married."

"You never married?" Lisa Mae's eyes, rimmed with all that black makeup, grew large. "You queer?"

"No. Busy."

"Never married, and no kids. Wow. I can't hardly imagine that. I'm on my second husband now, and Dickie is a good guy. I've got three kids, and he's got three, so together we've got us a houseful." She fished around in the pocket of her apron and came up with a pack of cigarettes and a plastic case full of photographs.

Laura was amazed that Lisa Mae would carry photographs of her kids in her pocket at work. But she did, and she unfolded them, and showed Laura the pride of her life, and seemed to delight in every one of Dickie's kids as much as her own. "I tell them, 'You learn to read, and you learn to cook, and you don't never end up down yonder.' Good advice, don't you think?"

Laura nodded. "If they can read, they can do anything."

"Yep. Wouldn't give 'em up for the world." Lisa Mae repocketed the photographs. "Sorry about your pa," she said. "And Charlie."

"Thanks."

"Charlie used to come in here for a cup of coffee with a tiny scoop of ice cream in it almost every day."

"He did?"

"A real gentleman, that Charlie." Lisa Mae's eyes turned sad. "Then he started having those fits. Your ma, sometimes she had to handle him all by herself, and that Charlie, he was a big guy."

"Fits? You mean seizures?"

"You know, cracked head and all."

Laura nodded, trying to imagine her tiny mother handling Charlie during a grand mal seizure.

"But you got kids, you do whatever it takes, that's for sure." Lisa Mae checked her watch. "I got to get back to work or I'll get my skinny ass fired. Let me bring you a piece of pie. Mo makes it fresh every morning, and it's good as it gets. My treat."

A moment later, a hot piece of apple pie with a scoop of ice cream landed on the table in front of Laura, along with a dispenser napkin and a fork, but Laura was still lost in the echoes of Lisa Mae's statement: "You got kids, you do whatever it takes."

Lisa Mae stayed in this town, married twice, raised her children, was personable and friendly to everybody, even those who treated her badly in high school. Laura never treated her badly, but Laura never liked her much, either. And Lisa Mae dealt with it. She didn't run away, abandon her heritage, she just lived with it. And here she was, friendly and giving and loving, to someone who had run away from home, someone who had denounced this jerkwater town, and Lisa Mae with barely a high school education.

And Laura, with all her fancy education, had left her tiny mother to deal with Charlie's seizures. And her brain-damaged father.

You got kids, you do whatever it takes.

You accept their brain damage, and you accept their abandonment.

Laura put a bite of pie into her dry mouth, swallowed it with the last of her coffee, left a ten dollar bill on the table, waved to Lisa Mae, who waved back, and stumbled for the door. She couldn't wait to get back to her mama. Laura had never learned to do whatever it takes. Her life was one selfish act after another.

Her mother's life had been one charitable act after another.

Guilt surged like bile. Maybe it wasn't too late to make restitution. Maybe it wasn't too late to figure it out. She drove fast back to the farm, but she drove carefully. She couldn't afford to be killed—or worse yet, injured enough so her mother would have someone else to care for—before she made amends. If she ever could make amends for the last twenty years.

She pulled into the drive amid a scattering of chickens, got out and ran to the front door. "Mama?" she called, but the house was quiet. The breakfast dishes had been done.

She put her purse on the kitchen table and went into the living room.

Whip was sleeping on the sofa, a game show playing softly on the television.

Laura walked into her mother's bedroom, but the bed was made and the room tidy.

"Mama?" she called upstairs, but there was no answer, so she walked up softly.

Her bed was neatly made. She walked into Charlie's room, and found it to be in perfect order, as well. *Sweet boy.* Her heart gave a painful squeeze. She looked at all the toys on his dresser, race cars, mostly, lined up by their mother on a lace doily. That had to be a new addition, Laura thought. She couldn't imagine Charlie living with doilies in his room.

The house was so clean. Neat and clean. And now that Laura thought of it, it had always been this way. Why did she always think of down yonder when she thought of home, instead of thinking of how fresh and scrubbed everything was inside her parents' house?

There was a stack of comic books on Charlie's nightstand. Laura sat for a moment on his bed, fingered the familiar bedspread, then picked up the comics.

Underneath them was a stack of Christmas cards.

Laura recognized them instantly, and a pang of grief threatened to double her over. She put the comics back down on top of the cards, went down the stairs and out the kitchen door, holding it back so it wouldn't slam and wake up her daddy.

The chickens ran over to see if she had any leftovers for them, but she just stood there, needing her mother, overwhelmed with emotion that she didn't know how to identify or to handle.

Then she saw a worn path through the weeds behind the house. She followed the path with her eyes and saw a small figure, cotton dress flapping transparently around the legs, standing on top of the ridge.

Laura started running.

~ ~ ~

Enid stood looking down on the mound of dirt that had begun to grow a good cover of weeds already. By the end of the season, nobody would ever know that Charlie was buried here, and that was probably just as well. He'd been a good man, but he came in mystery and he left in mystery and he lived a good, helpful, simple, loving life. It was fitting that he didn't leave much behind except those ripples of goodness. Enid thanked God that the town had no doctor, and the sheriff had actually come help her finish putting Charlie in the ground when Whip couldn't. No paperwork. Charlie had never had any paperwork to begin with, he sure didn't need any to end with.

"You just keep on making those angels laugh, Charlie boy," she whispered to him as she saw Laura come up the hill.

Laura was young and strong, stood straight and looked you right in the eyes. Enid could not be more proud, although she would rest a little easier if Laura were married, and had someone to take care of her. Women weren't meant to live alone and fend entirely for themselves. Life was to be shared, and while that wasn't always easy, it was really the only worthwhile thing.

Laura put an arm around Enid's shoulders, and they stood looking down at Charlie's grave for a long, silent moment.

"No marker?" Laura asked.

"Only in our hearts," Enid said.

Laura nodded, and Enid saw a drop darken a spot of dirt at her feet. Enid was cried out, but she was glad Laura had a chance to loosen up and expel a little phlegm of grief.

"I have to get back," Enid said. "Rufe Hoskins will be dropping by soon."

"Rufe Hoskins? What for?"

"The neighbors take turns coming by every day," Enid said.

"I don't even know my neighbors," Laura said with a catch in her voice.

"You could," Enid said, her arm tightening around Laura's waist.

Laura shook her head, her emotional glacier splitting and cracking right before Enid's eyes. "I don't know how."

"Well then," Enid said, realizing that missing her daughter's university graduation was nothing, now that she had an opportunity to see her daughter finish her real education, "come along and see Rufe. We'll show you."

Laura turned and wrapped her arms around Enid, and Enid felt those soft lips on her cheek, softer even than Charlie's. She held her little girl as long as she could, absorbing as much of that pain that she could, and then it was time to let the grief lapse for a time and go back to the real world.

"Bye, Charlie," she said. "See you tomorrow, honey."

"Bye, Charlie," Laura said.

"Can you bake a pie?" Enid asked her. "Your daddy loves a cherry pie."

"Teach me," Laura said, and took her mother's hand.

Don't Go

The darkness began to creep in around the edges of Blake's consciousness before he opened his eyes. Before Tara got out of bed. Before NPR began the 6 a.m. newscast.

Slowly, his muscles tightened. His fingers curled into fists as he lay quietly, feeling her move on the mattress next to him as she rubbed her face, pulled fingers through her hair, yawned. Stretched. Sighed.

"Good morning," she whispered, and ruffled his hair.

He gritted his teeth as he resisted reaching out and grabbing her by the wrist.

"Mmm," he said, his body rock steady, his face growing hot with the exertion to lie quietly.

Then she was up. He heard the shower run, the toilet flush, the buzz of the electric toothbrush.

He buried his face in the pillow. Soon she would come out of the bathroom, beautiful, her hair shining, her face perfect, her clothes stylish. And she would leave him, go out into the world to tempt the sickos who would have her all to themselves.

His medicine was on the nightstand, but he didn't want it. It flattened him out, turned him into a zombie, made him tolerate life, going through the motions of the day, not feeling, not caring. It sucked away all his passion.

It took care of the bad stuff, but it also took care of the good stuff.

He could take care of the bad stuff himself.

He slowly turned over onto his back, listening to her in the shower, imagining the shampoo suds gliding off her beautiful hair and down her back, across her athletic little butt and down those long legs. She'd rub the little bar of scented soap around her neck, her chest, her breasts, down that flat little tummy of hers, to the private place between her legs that he and only he had ever known.

Right? He had been her only lover, right?

A flush of uncertainty threatened to eject him right out of the bed and send him thrashing around the room in a rage.

Stop it!

He grabbed his head with both of his hands and squeezed.

Get control of yourself.

She had told him he was her first. Her only. He had no reason to doubt her.

Don't let her see you like this.

He relaxed back into the bed. Everything would be just fine.

"What's on your schedule today?" she asked, emerging from the steamy bathroom. A blast of perfumed mist surrounded her and he breathed it in. She smelled so girlish, so good. He opened his eyes. She stood next to the bed, combing out her wet hair, a green towel wrapped around her slim, tanned torso.

He forced a smile. "I'm not sure yet. I've got some calls to make, and then I'll work on my thesis."

"Isn't it due soon?" She squinted one eye and cocked her head. "This is February, hon."

I know exactly *what month it is.*

He relaxed his face with extreme effort and smiled at her. "That's one of the calls I need to make. I'm kind of stalled, waiting to hear from my advisor. I don't want to nag him, but I need to know if I'm on the right track."

"I'm sure you are. You're brilliant."

Brilliant.

He didn't care if he was brilliant. He wanted to be. . . everything. To her.

She dropped the towel, and he watched while she stepped into some blue striped panties and adjusted a matching bra with lace trim over those perfect breasts.

Heat came back up into his face. She should wear plain white underwear, like his grandma used to wear, just in case anybody got a glimpse, just in case she had an accident. What if she had to go to the emergency room and they cut away her clothing? Some stupid intern or orderly or something would see that lingerie—

But she had laughed at his paranoid suggestions. At first, she had laughed, it was so unlike him. But the darkness persisted, and then she got worried.

And then she threatened him. He needed help, she said. She couldn't live like this, she said.

He got help. He was using the help. But he didn't like taking the pills. He could control it himself. He was controlling it right now, wasn't he?

But it left no time to work on the thesis. And soon, she'd realize he'd stalled on it back in October, that he had not written a word since. He spent his days imagining the men who saw her all day long—men who spent their time scheming to steal her away from him, while he sat home, powerless. Agitating. Waiting to hear the sound of her key in the door.

Waiting until that moment when she got home, and she was his again.

Until the next morning.

They'd negotiated. He would stop following her. He would go to support group meetings. He would see a doctor. He would take the medication.

And in turn, she would stay.

"Have a little faith in me," she said, and kissed him tenderly.

It wasn't her that he was worried about. It was all those men out there. Men in her office, in her building. Men on the street, on the subway. There were men everywhere, men with evil intentions, men with bile in their hearts, who would take a beautiful woman like this and commit unspeakable crimes of cruelty and torture upon her.

Men who would crush her spirit with their control issues.

She put on thin socks, then stepped into a long wool skirt, pulled on and zipped up knee-high boots with heels and shrugged into a white cowl-neck sweater. She twisted her damp hair up and clipped it, then put on the pearl earrings he had given her on their second date and brushed on a touch of mascara and a bit of lip gloss.

She needed no makeup. She was the fresh-faced girl next door. She could be a model.

But of course he would never stand for that.

No, she was his model. His alone.

She snapped on her gold watch bracelet and gasped. "I'm late!" She took one last check in the mirror, then blew him a kiss from the bedroom door. "Have a good day."

"You'll be home. . ." He hated himself for asking.

"The usual time," she said, then smiled. Turned and disappeared. Looking perfect. Sensational.

Naïve. She was so naïve. She had no idea what kind of poisonous thoughts men held closely to themselves. She had no idea the kind of perverted fantasies she surely inspired in every man who saw her.

It was just a matter of time before one of them stole her.

And then what would he do? How would he live?

He wouldn't. He couldn't.

A moment later, the refrigerator door opened and closed. He pictured her putting the little container of yogurt and a banana into her bag. Breakfast. A few footsteps later, the front door closed behind her.

"Don't go," he whispered to the empty apartment.

But she was already gone.

～ ～ ～

Blake knew the drill. Get up, get showered. Call his sponsor and pour out all his fears. Listen to what Mitch said and do it. Turn his life over to the care of God as he understood God. Know that she was smart and resourceful and safe and coming home to him this evening.

Do not follow her.

Do *not* follow her.

But this was not a good day. This was a dark day where he had to lie flat on the bed, because to get up meant he would dress and go to her office and spy on her. He would make an excuse to see her inside her office, surprising her, and not in a good way. He would be there to follow her on her lunch break. He would hide around corners, and behind newspapers and all the corny things he saw people do in the movies.

Sometimes she caught him.

She couldn't catch him again, because then she would carry through on her threats, and he couldn't have that.

"What's this all about?" she'd finally asked, love and concern in her voice.

But he couldn't explain it. One day he just woke up to the fact that she was so precious to him that he couldn't live without her, and the fears began to take over him. Maybe it was the pressure of graduate school, or the mounting student loan debt with little chance of getting a good job with his master's in philosophy, or a million other things he began to worry about. But his fears seem to focus on his life after losing Tara, and they had escalated until they had virtually paralyzed him. "I don't know," he said, searching her eyes for clues to his behavior.

Was he picking up on subliminal messages that she was in fact cheating and hoping to get caught?

"Have a little faith in me," she had said.

"Have a little faith," his sponsor said.

Not today.

He lay spread-eagled on the bed, watching the clock, waiting for 5:17 p.m., the time, give or take three minutes, when she would walk through the door of their apartment, throw her bag on the couch, and give him a hug and a kiss.

He'd pull those boots off her glorious feet and she'd let him rub them while she told him about her day and he lied to her about his, fighting back tears of gratitude that she had actually come home to him one more time.

At 9:23, the phone rang. Blake turned his head and squinted at the caller ID. Mitch, his sponsor.

He didn't answer.

Tara was working at her desk with all those fresh-faced young executives seagulling around her, hoping for a glimpse of her smile, eager to bump into her, to catch the feel of her firm breast against an elbow. He needed to keep his intention strong, to surround her with his protection, to send her his strength.

At 10:47, he made his way to the bathroom, urinated, and brushed his teeth. She was making lunch plans. He didn't dare think of who she would be lunching with. Maybe today it would be some brilliant young mind with bright eyes behind fashionable glasses, freshly shaven and still smelling of his morning shower, with even white teeth, a Harvard MBA and a sense of humor that sent her into girlish giggles.

Blake used to be able to make her giggle like that.

He fell back into bed, thrashing, gripping handfuls of the sheet in sweaty hands and tried to think of something else. Anything else. A power greater than himself. That's what Mitch would be talking to him about, but Blake wasn't buying it.

At 2:51, he ate a piece of bread, misery turning it into sour, gummy dough in his mouth.

At 5:05, she was walking out the office door. Who held the door open for her? Did he ask her out for a drink? Was he too smooth to resist?

Blake leaped from his bed, and hurriedly threw the covers over the sweaty sheets.

She could not see him like this.

He jumped into the shower and quickly soaped up, not waiting for the water to heat. She'd be home by 5:17. He should look as if he'd been doing something all day instead of agonizing.

If she knew how he had really spent his day, she'd leave him.

But she wasn't home by 5:17, and he sat, still wet from the shower, clock in hand, staring at the digital numbers as they clicked by, desperate to hear her footstep outside in the hall. When the numbers clicked to 5:21, past the end of the three-minute window, he knew he'd lost her.

He dropped the clock on the floor in a deflating disappointment that transcended all other disappointment.

And he had only himself to blame.

He'd always been a loser, never worthy of her.

There was only one thing left to do.

Finally free from her, free from all the worry about her, feeling lighter than he had ever felt, he went into the bathroom, opened the cabinet and unzipped his travel kit. Two and three at a time, he swallowed the bottle of sleeping pills with handfuls of water from the sink, then retrieved the single-edged razor he kept stashed inside his shaving kit for just this inevitability.

For just this inevitability.

The time had come, at last.

As he had rehearsed a million times in his mind, he sat naked in the bathtub, and boldly took the first razor cut through the meat of his upper arm.

It didn't even hurt, and the red that poured forth felt cleansing.

The next cut was easier, on his inner thigh, and each one after that became easier still. Faster, and faster the razor slashed, and it felt so good to finally give vent to all his frustration over Tara, over the thesis, over his failures as a human being.

Let it out, let it all out.

Harder, deeper, faster, he kept at it, mesmerized by the sight, astonished at the lack of pain, feeling better with every slice until he looked up and saw blood spatters all over the shower tile. The bathroom looked like a slaughterhouse. Like a movie crime scene. Dizziness overcame him and the razor slipped from his trembling fingers to land on his leg and slip down somewhere beneath him.

He lay back in the bathtub, shivering, watching red liquid bubble forth from a hundred gashes, wishing he'd brought a blanket in with him. This was not a good way for the landlady to find him.

At 5:36, he heard her key in the lock.

Regret gripped him, but only for a moment. Regret was a much easier traveling companion than doubt.

She came home today, but what about tomorrow?

Maybe he should have talked to Mitch.

Maybe he should have given her more time.

Maybe he should have trusted her.

He watched from a long way away, understanding beginning to flower in his unencumbered spirit as she dropped her bag at the bathroom door, fell to her knees next to the bathtub, kissed his numb forehead and whispered the two heartfelt words he had never heard her say before. A thin sorrow colored his vision.

It was all too late now.

With a final backward glance, he saw her cradling his lolling head, smoothing his hair, whispering over and over the words he had so longed to hear her say.

"Please," she said. "Don't go."

But he was already gone.

Flying

When I was in high school, my father came to me in a dream. He held out his hand for mine, and said, "Let's go flying."

He'd been dead for a couple of years, and I missed him terribly, so when he showed up in my dream and wanted to spend time with me, I was more than eager. I grabbed his hand, and up we went, right through the ceiling of my room.

At first, I was startled, and then a little scared as we went higher and higher, and I clung to his hand with both of mine, but eventually I relaxed, as he was clearly not only experienced with this kind of thing, but completely in control of both of us.

We flew at treetop level over the woods by our house, and then higher and higher until we could look down and see the night lights of the city reflected in the river that wound through it. It's a view I'd seen in pictures, and from airplanes, but to be outside, in the fresh air, in the wind, with nothing on but my pajamas, the sight was magnificent. I grinned up at my dad and let go with one hand, so I could stretch out my arms. He smiled at me and we went even higher.

"See that little red spark down there?" he asked and pointed.

There were so many little red lights, taillights, streetlights, marquee lights, that I couldn't distinguish one from the other.

So he took me lower, and pretty soon I could indeed tell one red light that seemed different from the others.

"Those are seekers," he said. "Let's go mess with them."

We descended, not too fast, but steadily, until we were right on top of the house where the strange red light emanated.

Dad put his finger to his lips. "Shh," he said. I nodded.

We dropped through the roof, the attic and into a pink and white girly bedroom, where three young girls were sitting on the bed, candles on the nightstands, and a Ouija board in the middle. One of them had her fingers on the planchette. "Now concentrate," she said to her friends. "Ouija board, I want to know if Mario Rodriguez likes me. I mean, like, like-like, not just friends like."

Her two friends giggled. "*Mario Rodriguez?*" one of them whispered.

"Shush," the asker said.

My father reached over with his finger and moved the planchette vigorously around the board, and then stopped it pointing at the "Yes," in the corner.

The girl recoiled. "Oh my god!" she said. "Did you see that?"

"I saw you wanting it to tell you that Mario is in love with you."

"No, seriously," she said. "I didn't move it."

"Yeah, right."

"Here," she said, sliding the little heart-shaped piece of plastic to her friend. "You do it."

The second girl put her fingertips on the planchette. "This is so lame," she said.

"You have to take it seriously," the first girl said.

"Okay," she said, and sighed in resignation. "All right, Ouija board. Am I going to become rich and famous?"

The third girl scoffed and got two scowls, so she backed off.

"Rich and famous?" the girl asked again.

My dad grabbed the plastic thing with her fingers on it and began slowly moving it around the board.

"You're doing that," the third girl said.

"No, really, I'm not," the girl said, and pulled her fingers away. The planchette continued to move around and around and finally stopped at the "No" corner.

All three girls moved away from the board. The third girl said, "I don't think I want to play with this anymore."

"Me, neither," the never-to-be-be-rich-and-famous girl said. "It's stupid."

"It moved on its own!" the third girl said.

"It's real," the first girl said. "It's really real," she breathed with incredulity.

"You and Mario," the second girl sneered.

75

"Let's go," my dad whispered, and soon we were above the city again, soaring amongst the clouds which were misty on my face, but not at all cold.

The next thing I knew, it was morning, and I woke up in my bed, not at all certain of what had happened in the night, but I knew that my daddy still loved me and wanted to be with me, even if it was playing pranks on people in a dream.

It was probably two weeks before my dad came to me again, to take me flying. Every night, I was eager to go to bed, and every night I prayed that he would come, and every morning I was a little disappointed, but I had confidence that he would come back some time. And so he did.

This time he knew right where to go. There was no sight-seeing, and I immediately recognized the mysterious reddish light. We flew right to it.

This time it was an old house, and we floated through the walls to see seven people, eyes closed, sitting around a table, holding hands. One woman sat on a chair that was a little taller than the others; clearly she was leading this séance.

"Charlatan," my father whispered.

"I detect a presence," the woman said. "Someone who wishes to communicate with us from the other side is with us. "Speak," she commanded. "This is a safe place for you to express yourself."

My father picked up a corner of the table, held it up for a moment, and then dropped it. It hit the hardwood floor with a bang, and all the participants jumped, including me. Including the leader. She turned pale and looked around the room as if she could spot the irreverent one who dared to flaunt her authority. Her fraudulent authority.

"Who wishes to speak? I have pen and paper if you are more comfortable writing." The group calmed down and her hand began making circles around the paper, the penpoint not actually touching it.

My father grabbed her hand, put the pen point to paper, and wrote *I am Magnificent.*

The woman gasped. "Yes, yes," she said. "I agree, you are magnificent. What do you have to say to those here assembled?"

With a wink to me, he grabbed her hand again and wrote, *Go home and face your doom."*

"Okay," one woman said. She shook off the hands of the others, pushed her chair back and stood up. "I'm done with this."

"No, no, no," the leader said. "We're just getting started."

"You'll have to do it without me," she said. "This is bullshit." She grabbed her purse and coat from the back of her chair and stalked out.

My father looked at me with a gleeful satisfaction on his face. "Let's go," he said, taking my hand, and soon we were again soaring under the stars.

This experience, though, left a bad taste in my mouth. Didn't he have other, more important things to do? Didn't he have interesting things to teach me? I was so intrigued about the afterlife, so curious about revelations he had certainly had, but all he showed me was, quite frankly, what a jerk he could be. Had been, my whole life, truth be told. And now, actually, he was proving to those people that spirits do come from the other side of the veil to communicate. So that woman really wasn't a charlatan. He gave her credibility. Is this all there was to the afterlife? Playing tricks on gullible people?

This wasn't right, and I didn't think I wanted to do it anymore.

The next time he came, I wouldn't take his hand. He looked at me quizzically. "There must be more to the afterlife than this," I said.

"There is," he said. "But we also have time for fun. And this is fun." He paused. "Don't you think this is fun?"

"No," I said. "I like being with you, and I love the flying, but playing pranks on people is just kind of mean, I think."

His face clouded over in anger, a sight I was all too familiar with. "You were always weak," he said. "Looks like I'm going to have to teach you some lessons to toughen you up."

And then he was gone.

I woke up immediately, my insides on fire with emotions I had no words to express.

From that day on, I looked for the mean prank he would soon be playing on me. When my prom date stood me up, I looked at the sky, and said, "Is that you?" When my son broke his leg, I looked up and said, "Is that you?" When my husband got cancer, I looked up at the sky and said, "This is the cruelest prank of all, Dad. Is this you?" And a million other times while enduring pain.

And then when my hair turned gray and the veil became so thin that I could go back and forth at will, I saw him again, looking exactly as he had when I first went flying with him.

"Are you ready now that you've grown strong?" he held out his hand.

"I've grown," I said. "Have you?"

He nodded, and I saw the remorse in his face.

"I'm strong enough to do what's right," I said, "if you are." He nodded, so I took his hand and together we went soaring.

Hands of Heritage

Abraham Van Helsing watched out the window of his study until the shadow of the church steeple covered his father's grave. The old man still lay dead in the ground, and sheep grazed peacefully above him. Good.

Van Helsing rose from his chair with a wince at his arthritic hip and began to prepare for the coming evening. First, he put the teakettle to boil. He would need a stout pot. A long night lay ahead.

Mid-morning, the elder Craybourne boy had come to his door, out of breath and sweating, stinking like the pigs his family raised. His eyes were wide in his dirty face and his bad teeth showed in a fear-stretch of lip. "We found something, mister, me brother and me. Heard you'd pay."

"What?" Van Helsing had been disturbed from his morning reading, dozing in the sun, and was loathe to believe anything that came from the mouth of this cretin.

"You'll pay?"

"If the information is worthy. And reliable."

"Under the bridge," the boy said, trying still to catch his breath. "A whore of Satan."

"Oh?" Van Helsing stepped onto the porch. "Which bridge?"

"You'll pay?"

He reached into his pocket, pulled out a note and held it up. "Which bridge?"

The boy reached for the money, but Van Helsing lifted it slightly away from the outstretched hand.

"Halfway up the lane to the dairy," the boy said. "Acrost the creek."

"When did you see her?"

"Just now. Just now, me brother found her, came to me. I saw and came to you."

Van Helsing handed the boy the bill. The lad took it with grimy fingers and filthsplit fingernails, but instead of running off with his prize, he held the money tight in his fist and looked Van Helsing straight in the eye. "She killed me baby sister, I think," he said. "And a cousin."

Van Helsing nodded at the boy, and then he surprised himself by laying a hand on the damp boy's sticky shoulder. He shouldn't have done that. *He should never have done that.* He looked at that hand and it was the hand of his father.

He pulled it away, but it was too late. He'd seen the dreaded, familiar gesture, and now his hand stank and he couldn't even put it in his pocket. "All right then," he said, backed into the house and closed the door. He washed his hands carefully, staring into the mirror above the basin as he did so, then he thrust his hands, still damp, into black leather gloves and sat in his study to calm himself until the proper hour.

He watched the shadow of the steeple creep across the pasture, and when the shade encompassed the unmarked site of his father's rotting corpse, Van Helsing made his tea, drank it down, collected his tools and went out the front door. The evening air smelled fresh, in sharp contrast to the musty odor of his house, and Van Helsing made a mental note to tell the cleaning woman do a better job of airing it out.

The barn boy had readied the horse. Van Helsing mounted the gelding and set off toward the dairy at a walk. A gallop seemed too urgent, and a trot too merry for such a deed as was at hand.

The horse walked with a brisk and steady gate, as Van Helsing continued in vain to erase the memory of his hasty gesture and the look of his hand on the boy's shoulder. His father had used that friendly—or worse, *fatherly*—hand on the shoulder as a condescending gesture. The elder Van Helsing's hands had been distinctive in their pale softness. Not a single hard day's work had been accomplished by those hands; their only employment was to touch a shoulder, stroke a pen across a contract or a check, seal a negotiation with a shake. Mostly, those hands had been manicured and pampered, their perfect fingertips drumming impatiently whenever the father encountered the young Abraham's inquisitiveness or had to deal with the young Abraham's impetuousness. Those hands never touched Abraham with the respect of an equal. Not a handshake, not a pat on the back. Never. Abraham's accomplishments were invisible to his father, and there was nothing that would bring them to his attention.

He was a cold man, Van Helsing told himself, *and that is not your fault. You do not follow in his footsteps.*

But the hand—*his* hand—had looked exactly the same as his father's, soft and pale atop that young man's shoulder, and Abraham Van Helsing couldn't expunge the image from his mind.

The only thing that supplanted it from time to time as the horse carried him forward was the thought that perhaps a vampire was ripe for the killing under the dairy lane bridge. But that was doubtful. More likely the young fortune hunters had seen a rag washed up on a boulder, and their imaginations had run away with them.

He turned the horse up the lane, and with the bridge in sight, he began to rehearse his moves. The sun was lowering, yet still above; if there were a vampire, the thing would remain unconscious. He could kill her as she slept, but it worked to better advantage if she were wakening, groggy yet aware when he drove the stake through her.

It worked to his advantage.

Most importantly, it gave him the required satisfaction.

Abraham gave a small snort when his thoughts gave eloquence to that feeling. The required satisfaction, indeed. His life had hollowed out when his father died. All the meaning had evaporated with the old man's last breath. Abraham no longer had something to prove. Now he was immersed in his studies, uncaring about what the townspeople thought of him and his eccentric ways, and he was reduced to staking the undead for his personal satisfaction.

Oh, how his father would sneer.

Van Helsing snapped the reins, eager to be rid of these thoughts and on with the work at hand.

Shadows were long by the time Van Helsing got a grip on the she-demon's hair and dragged her out of the stinking, muddy culvert. She was just beginning to wake, her clothes ripped and threadbare, her breasts jiggling loose from their scrap of fabric. Van Helsing wished she were still asleep, so he could bathe her— clean her into the beautiful young woman she used to be. He remembered her; she had waited on him at the pub not more than six months ago.

But she could not be cleansed. She had the evil and was perpetuating it like a cancer throughout the countryside. She had to be stopped.

She moved groggily in his arms as he struggled to put her clothes right. It wouldn't do to be looking at her private places the way his traitorous eyes were drawn. He knew from a previous shameful experience that even though the lair of the vampire had a fetid stench, the thing itself had no personal odor. Even in that private place between her legs—so sweet on most women, fragrant and delicious—she was cold, sterile and lifeless. Her youth and beauty continued to attract the man in him, but the truth of her sacrilege could not be denied.

"Who's your maker?" he whispered in her ear as he pulled what was left of her dress down to cover. She groaned in response, flailing weakly. He laid her on the ground, then opened his sack and removed the sharpened stake and a hammer. The thing was regaining consciousness quickly as the sun disappeared over the western hills, and he had no time to waste. "Who's your maker?" he demanded.

Her eyes rolled back in her head, and she whispered a name. Against his better judgment, Van Helsing leaned closer to hear her, and when he did so, she grabbed his ear in her teeth and bit straight through it.

He yelled and pulled back, her teeth tearing through the flesh and cartilage of his ear. He pinned her to the ground with the stake at her breast. She growled. He put a knee on her belly, then took a firm grip on the hammer with his gloved hand and swung it.

The stake plunged deep. The thing screamed like a wildcat in heat, and then fainted.

Van Helsing, blood dripping down his neck from his torn ear, chided himself for being so careless. He finished pounding the stake, removed the head and stuffed the mouth with garlic. He left the corpse where it lay. He'd notify the constable who would find the girl's kin and see that she had a proper Christian burial.

When finished, he sat back and tended to his ear with a cloth damp from the muddy moisture of the stream. He looked at the poor woman before him and thought about her answer to his question. He thought for certain she'd said "Pater."

She must have said *"Peter."* It was a common enough name. There must be a dozen Peters in the county, but only one Pater. Pater Van Helsing, Abraham's father. Pater died of brain fever two years ago and had been safely buried in the churchyard with full Christian regalia. The bishop had seen to it. It had been Abraham's worst nightmare that his father fall victim to the relentless plague of vampirism that scourged the English countryside.

It was unthinkable that Pater was a vampire, a vampire who controlled the young thing in the ditch under the bridge. Inconceivable. From the study window, Abraham viewed his father's grave every day of his life, and it remained undisturbed.

He groaned to his feet, repacked his valise, and one hand to his injured ear, he mounted the gelding and made for town. First to see the constable, and second to the doctor for some stitches. Since he had killed the monster who bit him, he would not be infected with vampirism. He had other things to worry about. He replayed her whispered response to his question over and over again, and mentally reviewed the symptoms of his father's fatal fever, and by the time he reached town, Van Helsing had become convinced that he had heard the woman correctly: *his father remained undead.*

The next day, Abraham and the parish bishop watched the two Craybourne boys lift Pater Van Helsing's casket from its grave. Abraham held his breath as the eldest Craybourne pried open the coffin.

Empty.

Darknesss swirled in the periphery of Abraham's vision, and his knees weakened. The bishop helped him to the ground where he took deep breaths and tried to imagine the ramifications of this discovery. Then he tried to imagine where his father might lie during the day. He had to be found. Abraham had to put an end to the scourge. He had to find his father and stake him, cut off his head and fill the mouth with garlic. And then he had to find the vampire who had infected Pater and do the same to it.

Abraham felt old, tired, and ill-equipped for the task that lay ahead. He closed his eyes and rested his forehead on his knees. He thought he had been finished with his father forever once that coffin had been lowered into the graveyard and dirt thrown atop it. And now this.

And now this.

That night, he dreamed his father appeared at his bedside. Pater seemed to materialize out of stardust, and the years that had ravaged his ancient body had fallen away, leaving a young Pater Van Helsing—handsome and stylish, but with a new intensity foreign to Abraham. "My son," he said. "My son, why do you waste your life? All your education, all your gifts and talents, all the good work you've done in the world. Rest now and enjoy your retirement. Leave the distasteful jobs for the young and energetic. Go home to Amsterdam and leave these ridiculous English to themselves. Rest now.

Rest." Then as he had materialized, he swirled away into the moonlight, leaving Abraham to wonder if it was a dream or the evil of Dracula whose wretched spawn still thrived.

Abraham tried to imagine the act of staking his own father, and he couldn't. The hot ball of emotion in his chest pushed tears out his eyes.

There would be no rest for him this night.

There may never be rest for him again.

The next day, the exhaustive search began. Every spare person gathered at the town square: the women, the unemployed, the retired, the aged. The bars and schools were closed. Abraham beseeched them to seek, find and report the vampire's lair. He encouraged them to bejewel themselves with crucifixes and to store holy water in their homes. But most importantly, to look everywhere a body might lie in darkness. In the attics, under the houses, in the crypts, in the woodsheds, the factories, barns, everywhere, *everywhere*.

As he spoke, Abraham knew he was panicking the simple folk, but there was nothing to be done about that. They would have to come to terms with their own fears eventually, and the sooner they found the beast, the quicker the panic would be over. "The stench of a vampire's lair is unmistakable," he said to them. "Fetid guano. Ammoniac. Follow your noses."

Immediately, of course, the fearful peasants began describing an unceasing stream of stinking spaces. Each had to be investigated, and nowhere was found the undead corpse of his father. As the search passed from weeks into months, Abraham's energy failed along with his will, and despite all his efforts and those of the townspeople, the occasional young, raven-haired woman still disappeared. Each one bore a heart-wrenching resemblance to Abraham's long-dead mother.

The only solace for Abraham's torture was the company of the bishop, now retired, whose council Van Helsing cherished. The bishop visited for a glass of sherry every evening to keep abreast of the search, doing his best to tsk-tsk and shake his head at the apparent wily nature of Van Helsing's cunning, elusive prey. Van Helsing thought the bishop would be more involved, the evil being what it was, right under his own nose, in his own parish, but the bishop seemed to be interested only in the progress of the hunt and emotional and mental state of Van Helsing himself. As they talked of an evening, the bishop showed an undue interest in the spiders who came in from the cold to nest quietly in the corners of Van Helsing's den. They seemed drawn to him, and he let them crawl about on his hands and arms while Abraham talked of the hunt.

Then early one morning, after a sleepless night, as Van Helsing considered booking passage back to Amsterdam and leaving England and all it had failed to offer him, the bishop barged into his house. He grabbed Abraham's wrist, and with urgency and a madness in his eyes, said, "Leave, Abraham, I beg of you. Immediately! You are not safe! None of us are safe! I can resist him no longer!" And with that, the man suffered a terrible seizure and collapsed on the foyer floor.

Van Helsing called for the barn boy to fetch the doctor, but by the time that order had been delivered, the bishop had been delivered of his soul.

Van Helsing fell into his chair in front of the fire, emotionally overwrought. His health was not pampered by the foggy dampness of the English winter. He was not a young man, and the search for the creature his father had become was taking what could be a mortal toll. So it had been on the bishop.

Vampires were sly. Van Helsing remembered Renfield, the mental patient who had been Count Dracula's lackey, and the similarities to the bishop were no longer to be ignored.

Neither was that stink that permeated his house as it leaked up through the floorboards.

My God, he thought. *The devil resides beneath my very own home.* He was incensed that the creature had been privy to all their searching through the conduit of the bishop, a supposed holy man. Van Helsing had felt safe and confident in his own home and had enjoyed the bishop's company. The double deception sliced him deeply.

He finished his tea—in no hurry to decapitate his own father—and then assembled his kit. When the barn boy came back with the doctor, they helped him rip the boards off the north side of the house. All three nearly retched at the stench that poured forth. Van Helsing steeled himself and crawled into the darkness, dragging his willpower along with his valise of tools.

There Pater lay under the floorboards, a handsome young man, his lips red and engorged and a trickle of some young woman's blood still at the corner of his mouth. He looked very much like Abraham had in his youth. The demon virus had at least restored Pater's looks if not his health and vitality. Abraham tugged at the old blanket the monster slept on, hoping to drag it into the burning sunlight before he plunged the stake, but the space was too cramped, the body too heavy, and Abraham too weak of will. He took the freshly sharpened stake from his bag and placed it carefully on the thing's chest. He put a knee on its bloated stomach and raised the hammer.

Pater Van Helsing opened his eyes just as the hammer struck home and the stake plunged into his heart. Abraham searched those eyes for a brief glimpse of humanity, hoping to find some. Hoping to find none. Hoping to find forgiveness and hating himself for needing it. This one did not scream and writhe like most of the other vampires Abraham had staked. It just stared at him with a faint flicker of recognition.

He quickly retrieved the machete from his bag and severed the head of Pater Van Helsing, then sat back, viewing his wretched work, loathing himself and the unnamed force that drove him to this life, this vocation.

Abraham lifted his hands in front of his face. He'd forgotten his gloves and his father's blood dripped from his fingers and ran down his wrists to his elbows.

His father's hands had never seen such work. Such filth.

Such pride.

"These are my hands," he said softly. At that moment, he knew that what he had become was nothing to be ashamed of in the face of what his father had ultimately become. Then louder, as if to convince the sightless corpse that lay in front of him: "Behold!" he said to it. "*These* are *my* hands!"

Honing Sebastian

Sebastian found the paper sack at 0217 hours on Monday, the sixteenth of Aout, the day of our Lord Hammersmith 12. He saw it in the corner of the doorway of an old apothecary and made note of all the details in his journal before he approached it.

He expected it to be empty, something blown there from the other world, but when he touched it, he could tell it had weight. He made note of that in his journal, along with the words that were printed in green on its side. The words made no sense to him, but he copied them as exactly as he was able.

Then he looked inside the sack, and the terror seized him. He cringed, hunkered down over the sack, expecting to hear sirens. He expected the great hands to grab him, rough fingers bruising him, lifting his bony body off its feet and carried by burly, faceless, hairy creatures in blue to throw them into a caddy and land him on concrete with four walls.

But no sirens. No caddy, no blues. He gave a furtive look both ways down both sides of the street, then tucked the bag inside his trou.

Then he made a note of it, but he didn't note what he saw inside it, and all the way home, the pencil stub and his journal glowed white hot in his pocket with the omission. The rents would want to know what he didn't note. They could see into his mind. They'd see that he hadn't written everything down, as were his orders, and he would be punished.

But he didn't think the rent punishment would be worse than the blues, so he took his chances.

Now that, too, was a thought he ought to write down, but couldn't. Maybe he needed a different journal. One to write down the things he showed to the rents, and one he kept for himself. Because he not only felt the stub and the notebook glowing in his pocket, so was the bag in his underwear. He could hear it, too, with every step. He crouched lower, and told it to hush quietly, but he didn't think it heard him. It didn't have to. It was too valuable. It could think whatever it wanted, be as loud as it wanted, and nobody would care. It could scream, shriek, be vulgar, and still everybody would want it. Especially the rents and the blues.

But Sebastian had found it, so it was his. He'd have to keep it secret from the rents *(A secret from the rents!)*.

But then, he wondered, as he neared the D, what good was it if he couldn't let others know he had it? By itself, it wasn't valuable at all. It was only valuable when others knew he had it. That's what would give him the power.

He ought to write that down. Not for the rents, for himself. In the alternate notebook.

Why had someone left it in the bag in the doorway, anyway?

Maybe it wasn't real.

Sebastian scuttled past the D, all the way to the river. The fire wasn't so big today, but still there was enough smelch for him to hide inside it for a few minutes. This was where he came to do his secret things. He had secrets he'd never told the rents. Maybe that's why this was so easy. Sometimes he came to the river to talk to himself, and sometimes he put his hands in his pants, and sometimes he talked to the rents in a whisper, when he was certain nobody else could hear him. He was a sinner.

This time, enshrouded in the black acrid smoke, Sebastian pulled the bag from his underwear, opened it up and looked in again.

The sight of it scared him, and he had to keep himself from flinging it into the burning river, or shoving it back into his trou. He needed to look at it, to touch it, to handle it, to make certain it was what he thought it was.

It was. Riches far beyond his imagination. Oh, what he could do with this.

He ought to make a note.

But he didn't.

Instead, he talked to himself, he talked to the rents, he put his hands in his pants, and when he went back to the D, he was a sinner for certain.

"Whereya been?" Slicer asked as soon as Sebastian ducked inside. "You stink."

"River." Sebastian was certain now that not only did his journal and stub glow, but so did the bag and so did his face. He was going to lie to Slicer, and some day she'd find out and hate him.

"Why?"

He pushed her out of his way and walked quickly past the tattooing, then slid down the pipe into the tube, then, not hearing her behind him, began to run along the tracks. He'd never run before that he could remember; nobody ran, especially down here in the dark. But Sebastian ran, and he liked the way it made his lungs and legs hurt.

His blanket was in a safe zone; the rents never went this far out, although Slicer and the rest of the hoons did. The young ones were thieving, vandalizing little shits, so Sebastian never left anything there but his blanket. They didn't want his blanket; they wanted valuable things. Sebastian never had anything of value; just his old journals, and they were only valuable to him because the rents would be mad at him if he didn't produce the current one on demand. And it better be up to date. Up to the minute, even.

Once back at his blanket, Sebastian sat with his back in the corner of his nook, his stomach rumbling. He'd forgotten to find grinds after he'd found the sack. Now he had to decide where to hide *(hide!)* the sack and its magic from the rents and the hoons. He had no idea how to even begin to go about it.

He wrapped up in his blanket, listening to the dark wind blow through the tunnel. The wires vibrated and sang with songs of long ago, and sometimes Sebastian hummed along, matching their tone.

But not today. Today Sebastian needed to search his soul. He had to decide if he was going to defy convention and embrace sin, or if he was going to confess, take his punishment, and slip back into anonymity.

He kind of wanted to search his soul, but he already knew what he was going to do. He just had to get his courage up. And figure out how to hide the bag.

The papers were real; he'd seen enough of them. Occasionally a hoon found one and one of the rents snatched it away. This was a whole bundle of them. Big, fat, heavy bundle. The rents would want it. The other hoons would want it. He wanted it. He wanted to go up with it, into the street, and become a civilian. He could wear real linen, he could grind real food, he could walk in the sunshine.

He'd seen sunshine; he'd seen the civilians wandering around in it as if it were free for the taking. Perhaps it was for them, but it could never be for

Sebastian. He wore the black. He had the tattoos. He lived underground. "As it has been, so will it be." That's what the rents said, quoting the Hammersmith.

But now he had the means to pay his way.

"Hey." Slicer climbed up onto his ledge, startling him. "Whatcha doin'?"

Slicer had a way of sneaking up, her clothes black against the dark, hair black, face smudged, hands and forearms tattooed, rending her almost invisible, which worked to her advantage. The whites of her blue eyes shone bright in the dimness, and Sebastian could see her hair shining yellow where it had grown in at the part. Yellow, like sunshine.

"Thinking about sunshine," Sebastian said.

"We could go tomorrow," Slicer said.

"Into the sun?"

"I go every day."

"You lie," he said in disbelief. "How?"

"You think I tell the rents everything?"

Sebastian nodded. This idea of withholding things from the rents was a brand-new concept to him, but apparently not to everybody.

"Well, I don't." She picked at a ragged fingernail.

"What don't you tell them?"

"That I go up there and walk with the civvies."

"The civvies let you?"

"They don't stop me."

"What about the rents?" he asked.

"What about them?"

"They'll read your mind."

"They can't," Slicer said.

"They can. They took Tukki and read her mind and then punished her for blasphemous thoughts. She told me."

"Tukki's a tweeb," Slicer said. "She should die."

Sebastian knew there was more that Slicer wasn't telling him. He was amazed that she walked in the sunshine with the civvies. That was blasphemous. Punishable. "What else?"

Slicer put her hand in her lap and looked him square in the eye. "I found my family again," she said. "And sometimes I visit them."

Sebastian was astounded at this news. "Then why do you live down here?"

"I don't think they want me," she said, and went back to torturing the fingernail.

"Do you grind with them?"

She shook her head.

"Talk?"

Again, she shook her head no.

"Do they see you?"

"No, but—"

"Then how do you know they're your family?"

"Because I want them to be."

Sebastian had such an overwhelming feeling of affection for Slicer that he almost revealed his secret to her. He had a moment of clear fantasy where they went upstairs together, lived like civilians, had a baby, played with it in the sunshine. On grass. The words were on the tip of his tongue. He was about to take her hand and tell her that they could do that, they could make a family just like the one she wanted to be hers, the two of them, but then she opened her mouth one more time, and the illusion, the dream, evaporated like a wisp of riverfire smelch.

"Dicks and I are running away together," she said. "We're going to Hollywood."

Sebastian pulled away from her and hugged his blanket. He hoped his hurt and disappointment didn't show. "When?"

"Now. I come to say goodbye."

"I'll miss you," he said, and meant it. A hot ball of emotion stuck in his throat and he couldn't say anything more.

She reached forward and wrapped her arms around his neck, then up on their knees, she pressed her body next to his.

The bag in his crotch crinkled. Sebastian hoped she hadn't heard it.

"What's that?" she asked, pulling back.

"What?"

"That noise. What's in your trou?"

"Nothing."

"Don't lie."

"Don't tell anybody."

"As if I would," she said.

He trusted her. She went to the sunshine. She and Dicks were leaving, breaking *all* the rules. He trusted her and he loved her. Maybe if she saw the swag, she'd stay with him. They could escape together into the sun. The fantasy was back.

91

He reached into his trou and brought out the bag.

"Hammers," she said. "Did you note it?"

"Yeah," Sebastian said, "but not what was in it."

"What?"

He opened the bag and let her look inside. Before he could stop her, she reached inside and pulled out the papers.

"Hammers, Sebastian, you're rich."

"Come with *me* to the sunshine, Slicer." He felt suddenly desperate. He'd shared his secret, and now he wanted to share its fruits. Being rich was no good alone. "Forget Dicks. We'll be our own family. We'll have a baby."

She looked at him with surprise in her eyes. "A baby," she whispered. Then with an anger he'd never known from her before, she ripped the bag out of his hands. "You stupid," she said, jumped off the ledge and ran off down the tube. Sebastian listened to her footfalls echo as far as the D, and then he couldn't hear them anymore. He was alone with the black wind that blew down the tunnel and right through his heart.

Sebastian stayed curled up with his blanket for longer than he ever had before. His heart was broken—he could feel the sharp edges cutting haphazardly inside his chest, he could hear the pieces rattle around when he got up and went down the tunnel to make. He didn't grind. He didn't talk. He saw no sun. He had no dreams. He just lay with his blanket and let his eyes leak.

Now and then one of the hoons, or occasionally a small gang of them, came around and tried to roust him, but Sebastian had nothing to say to them. They could rob him of…of…of what, his pencil? He didn't care. They could beat him and he didn't care. They could kill him and that would be good. But they didn't. They just poked at him and when he didn't respond, they wandered off.

Sebastian wanted Slicer back. He wanted the papers back. He wanted the power—no, he wanted the dream. There was a dream inside him that shone forth for a quick minute, and then it was gone, and he missed it.

But as he lay there, cold against the concrete, he began to think of Hammersmith, and why he would give Sebastian a dream and then deny him. That part didn't make any sense. Perhaps Sebastian had been too long without grinds, but he thought that maybe the rents were wrong.

More blaspheme, Sebastian, he told himself, but he didn't care anymore. He didn't care about the rents, he didn't care about himself, he didn't care about anything. Just when he decided that he'd go into the sun and ask a civilian his question about the dream and the rents and Hammersmith, a hoon raced by. "Rents!" he shouted, and Sebastian's heart began to pound. Rents? This far out? Why?

He pulled his legs up underneath him, wrapped his blanket around them, and tried to make himself invisible squenched into the corner of his nook. It wasn't long after the hoon came by that he heard footsteps coming down the tube, and even though it was dark, he could see the rent's face. It was as if he had his own light, he was so clean and white.

"Sebastian?" the rent said with a soft voice, and Sebastian thought he was going to faint at the sound of it. He scrambled for his journal, the most recent one—but he hadn't noted anything in it since that day he found the bag.

"Aye," Sebastian said.

"Are you sick?"

"No."

"We heard you were sick."

"No." Sebastian couldn't stop trembling.

"Stand up."

Sebastian stood, but his trou threatened to fall to his ankles, so he gripped them. His knees shook. The rent had a kind face. This was not like any of the rents he'd ever seen before, with their hooked noses, red hair, and hard, evil mouths.

"When was the last time you ate?"

"Ate?"

"Grinds."

"Don't know."

The rent held out a brown paper sack. "Here," he said. "Don't tell anybody I gave you this."

"Tell who?"

"Anybody. Hoons. Rents."

Sebastian cowered until the rent placed it on the ground at his feet. Then the rent smiled and turned away.

Sebastian could smell grinds in the bag. They made his stomach grumble. They made his mouth water. But this rent, this was not an ordinary rent. This was a civilian. He could ask his question.

"Dreams?" he said to the man's back. "What about dreams?"

"Dreams?" the man turned back around. "What kind of dreams?"

Sebastian couldn't answer. His mouth was befuddled with the emotion in his throat. His eyes began to leak and he hicc'ed and couldn't catch his breath. "Dreams of sunshine," he finally choked out. "Babies on the grass."

"We are made of dreams, Sebastian," he said. "Is that yours?"

Sebastian began to sob. He stood, holding up his trou, water running down his face, and nodded. He felt more pitiful than ever.

"Anything else?"

"Slicer."

"Slicer?"

"She's a hoon."

"Ah," the man said. "Love. Good." He held out his hand. A soft, white hand with clean fingernails that seemed to glow of its own accord in the darkness. "Well, come on, then."

Sebastian was confused. "Am I dead?" he asked.

The civilian laughed, and his white teeth flashed like Slicer's. "Soon enough. C'mon."

"Trust?"

"That's part of your dream, isn't it?" the man said.

Sebastian put his skinny, dirty, tattooed hand into the man's, and jumped down off his ledge, leaving his blanket and his journals. "I had power one time," he said.

"I believe you, son."

Sebastian, his heart filled with a hope he'd never known, walked next to the big man down through the tube, but instead of ducking into the D, they kept walking, all the way to the light stairs. Sebastian had never been to the light stairs before. He knew about them, of course, but up those stairs is where the rents lived out their miserable lives and none of the hoons wanted anything to do with them, much less enter their territory on purpose. It wasn't so much that nobody wanted anything to do with them, it was more that everybody was afraid of them. Sebastian was certainly afraid. The rents had mystical powers. The rents could pull information right out of your mind. Sebastian didn't want anything pulled out of his head.

Sebastian hung back. "Rents," he said, and nodded toward the stairs.

"It's okay, boy," the man said. "You're with me. Remember your dream."

Sebastian's heart beat so hard in his chest that he found it difficult to breathe. The man took his hand again, and pulled him along, pulled him almost against his will, to the stairs, and then up them, one at a time. Almost against Sebastian's will, but not quite. Sebastian was afraid, but intrigued. Could the dream be on the other side of the door at the top of the stairs?

Could a black-clad, tattooed hoon ever really go into the light? Or was he doomed to live like a rat in the tunnels, foraging for grinds and a pittance to hand over to the rents so they wouldn't hunt him down and beat him?

There were a few old hoons, but not many. There were lots of old civilians. Sebastian looked up at the man beside him, in the faint light cast by the magic stairs, and he saw the civilian's gray hair and lined face. This was no hoon. This was a champion.

Sebastian pulled his hand from the man's, took a deep breath, straightened his back, tossed his hair and took the stairs of his own free will. They'd take him to hell or they'd take him to freedom, and he was soon to find out which.

At the top, the man pulled out a key and opened a heavy door. They stepped into a stinky corridor with light emanating from an indeterminate source. Sebastian could hear someone crying.

"This way," the man said, and Sebastian, feeling small and weak again, uncomfortably out of his element, followed. They went through a series of light corridors, stairs and doors, and finally opened a glass door and stepped into a bright room with big windows on the street that let in all kinds of light. It hurt Sebastian's eyes.

"What's this, Leo," an older woman said, peering over half glasses at Sebastian, "something the street vomited up?" She looked like a rent with her gold earlobes.

"This is Sebastian," the man said. "He has a dream."

The woman cackled, and Sebastian wanted to shrink, to turn back, to run back to the safety of his blanket. It seemed as though the man was making fun of him. He felt hot nose water run down onto his upper lip and spread out through his thin mustache. He wiped at it with the back of one hand, while the other held onto his trou. He wanted to guard his head so she couldn't pull information out. He didn't want her to know about Slicer going to Hollywood with Dicks and the bag of papers.

The man shuttled him through the room full of furniture and papers and into another little room with a soft place to sit. He closed the door behind him and they both sat down.

"So far so good, Sebastian?" the man asked.

Sebastian nodded. He wondered if this man was a rent in disguise.

"I'm going to help you find your dream, Sebastian. Do you believe me?"

Sebastian nodded. The man hadn't locked the door. If he felt his mind being invaded, he could just run.

"Do you know what makes people sick, Sebastian?"

Sebastian shook his head.

"Doing the wrong thing."

Here it was. Sebastian felt the rents creeping inside his skull.

"Doing things that aren't right. Stealing. Lying. Not carrying your share of the load. Do you know what I'm talking about?"

Sebastian's muscles tensed. He nodded at the man, trying to understand how he could look so nice, yet be an enemy.

"Is there anything you'd like to tell me?"

Sebastian shook his head.

"Confession, Sebastian, is what the soul craves. Unburden yourself, because if you're ever going to find your dream—"

They knew he was hiding. It was too late. If he didn't say something, they were going to suck it out of his head. "Slicer stole my swag and went to Hollywood with Dicks," he blurted out.

The man nodded. "We know about them," he said. "They're not in Hollywood. They're right here. Safe. Like you."

Sebastian exhaled a sigh of relief. He felt better. The man was right. He felt lighter, unburdened. That was what they wanted from him, then. He could go. He stood up, felt like he stood a little taller, even though he'd ratted out his girl. "I'm going," he said.

"Know who the rents are, Sebastian?"

No, Sebastian did not know who the rents were. He sat back down. This might be valuable information.

"Tenants. They pay rent on this building we're in. Know who they pay rent to?"

Sebastian shook his head. He wasn't certain he understood all of this.

"Me. I have an enormous cash-eating machine that requires a lot of income. Wives. Airplanes. Swimming pools. Know where my income comes from?"

Sebastian suddenly knew where this was going, and he was afraid. He wanted to throw himself on the floor and kiss the man's shoes. Sebastian knew who he was talking with, but he didn't want anyone to utter the name. The holy name.

"My income comes from the tenants. They get their income from you folks, who work the streets for them. Know your place in the hierarchy? There are crows and vultures in the natural world, Sebastian, who clean up the roadkill. Carp keep the streams clean. Worms recycle earth nutrients. You and the hoons pick the streets clean every night. Sometimes things of value are passed to the rents, who pass them on to me. So see? Your place in the world is part of *my* dream. I need you, Sebastian. And Slicer and Dicks and the rest. But I'd like my dream to be your dream, too."

Sebastian felt a little bit calmer. What the man was saying was making a strange sort of sense. He felt like maybe he had a defined place in the world after all. He relaxed.

"I need you to keep doing what you're doing. You make a tremendous contribution to the rents, to me, to the city, to the other hoons. You provide jobs and income. You and the others, Sebastian, you're the ones that make the whole system work. Do you see what I'm saying?"

Sebastian nodded.

The man put a soft white hand on Sebastian's shoulder. "When Slicer and Dicks decided to go to Hollywood with the bagful of money, they were disrupting the system, and the system can't be disrupted if it's to work right. We can't have crows killing raccoons, now, can we?"

Sebastian didn't understand that, exactly.

"So I need you to go back to work, keeping your journal, reporting everything you see and hear, for the betterment of society, Sebastian. All of society. We each have our place in it. And now do you how to make your dream come true?"

Sebastian shook his head.

"When you make your reality your dream. Understand?"

Sebastian sort of did. He nodded.

"Good boy," the man said. "I'm sorry about your friends, but if you walk the straight and narrow, just as the rents ask of you, you'll be leading the good life. The life that was laid out for you to live. It's important what you do. Your actions have value to me and to the others. Okay?"

Sebastian nodded.

The man stood up and offered Sebastian his hand. Sebastian shook it. "If you have any more questions, son, come to the light stairs and ask for me. I'm Leo. Leo Hammersmith."

Tears choked Sebastian again, and he couldn't speak. He was in *the presence.*

Hammersmith showed him out and gave him vague directions as to how to get back to the light stairs.

Sebastian stumbled his way along. When he got to the place in the corridor where he could hear the crying, he recognized the voice. Slicer.

But he couldn't help her. He had a job to do.

Persistence Pays

Lois looked at the three women, each with a glass of white wine, each dressed in a little black cocktail dress, comfortable for the balmy evening on Brice Bickert's patio. But there the similarity ended. Kirsten, young, innocent, wide-eyed and blonde, who looked like the girl next door, Stephanie, tall and brunette, with red lips and a vixen's stare, and Angela, tattooed, fried red hair, green glossy eye shadow and dark painted brows. And Lois. Older. Married. Successful. Tailored. Four women, not far apart in age, each well put together, each seemingly happy, smart, successful, connected. Each at Brice's birthday party. It would seem they had much in common, although what Lois was hearing was far beyond the scope of coincidence, much less common. Lois, obviously the eldest, found herself inexplicably gravitating toward the three women, and once they began to discuss their backgrounds, the conversation became too eerie to dismiss.

"It's uncanny," Lois said, and the four women took another step closer to each other and peered into one another's faces. "Sixteen twelve?"

Three nods.

"Pheasant Trail Lane?"

Three nods.

"In White Pines Junction? Jeez, you're kidding, right?"

"Brick two story," Stephanie said with a flip of her brown hair.

"Attic with a round leaded window," the youngest Kirsten said, blue eyes growing wider.

"Scary fucking basement," Angela the tough broad said, with her poorly capped teeth, and she knocked back the last of her scotch.

"Let's sit down," Lois said, not exactly trusting her knees, or her ears,

99

and wanting to put her wine aside so she was completely in charge of herself during this investigation. They followed her to a table on the lawn set with tea lights. Once seated away from the party, they all fell shy in the long July dusk.

"It's not just uncanny," Stephanie whispered. "It's too weird."

"When did you live there?" Lois asked, unable to keep the disbelief from her voice. She'd lived in that house from the moment she was born until 1962, so if any of the others' claims conflicted with that, she'd know she was being put on by somebody. Brice, probably. This was a Brice-type prank.

"Sixty-two to sixty-eight," Angela said.

"Sixty-nine to seventy-nine," Stephanie said.

"Seventy-nine to eighty-four," Kirsten said, and looked at Lois expectantly.

"Jesus," Lois said. It was a stunning revelation, but if it wasn't Brice, then it was clearly Vargas County. She'd moved far away from White Pines Junction, and still its tentacles reached out to touch her.

"I need a fresh drink," Angela said, but made no move toward the house.

"What are we going to do?" Stephanie asked.

"Do? About what?" Angela replied. "There's nothing to do."

But Lois knew what Stephanie meant. They'd been assembled for a reason. Coincidences like this just did not happen without an expected action.

"Brice put you guys up to this, right?" Angela said, then looked around as if she was expecting a waiter to bring her a fresh Scotch.

Ignoring her and taking charge because she was obviously the eldest and being in charge was second nature to her, Lois said, "We have to go there."

"No," Kirsten said. "Never."

"Nope," Stephanie said.

"Only to watch it burn," Angela said.

"Next weekend," Lois said, and in spite of themselves, they all nodded.

~ ~ ~

A week later, they sat in Lois' rented Taurus in front of sixteen-twelve Pheasant Trail Lane. It was strange, Lois thought, how they were all available to fly all the way across the country, arrive at approximately the same time, meet at the rental car desk without a hitch, and drove all the way north together without a squabble. Well hell, there were a lot of strange things going on. And now here were four women who didn't know each other, sitting in front of an old house, each of them a former resident of this exact same house, and nobody wanted to go inside.

Someone or something else was pulling the strings here, and she didn't know what to do except try to cooperate.

"Looks empty," Stephanie said.

"Run down," Kirsten said.

"I need a drink," Angela said.

"It is empty," Lois said and held up a key. "The realtor sent me this." She unbuckled her seat belt. "C'mon."

She opened the door, and the women stepped into a hot, musty, close living room with brown carpet and gold wallpaper.

Kirsten was the first to react. "Oh, God," she said, "that smell! I can't take that horrible smell." She covered her nose and mouth and looked like she was about to gag.

"I don't smell anything," Lois said. "What does it smell like?"

"Like rotten meat. Decaying things. God, I can't stand it."

"Come on," Lois said, pulling on her elbow.

"I can't," Kirsten said, and sank to the floor. "I'm going to puke."

"Jesus, don't sit on that carpeting," Stephanie said. "You have no idea what's been done—what's been—you know, spilled on it."

"What happened to you here?" Lois asked Kirsten, sitting on the floor next to her.

"I think the smell is coming from the attic," Kirsten said.

"Let's go look," Angela said.

"No!" Kirsten said. "You can't go up there. Nobody can. Jake doesn't want you up there. Jake doesn't want us to be here."

"Jake?" Lois asked, and her insides took a tumble.

"My brother," Kirsten sobbed.

"My brother," Angela said.

"*My* brother," Stephanie said.

"Good God," Lois said. "He was *my* brother, too."

With that, Angela opened her purse and pulled out a flask.

"So that's why we're here," Lois said, marveling. "Jake has called us all home."

"Wait a minute," Stephanie said. "How could we all have the same brother? We're not related."

Angela shrugged. "How could we all just meet at Brice's?"

"That could be a coincidence," Stephanie said. "But this—this is biology."

"Well," Lois said, "I remember when Jake was born. I was six."

"My brother Jake died when I was four," Stephanie said.

"Can somebody open a window or something before I puke?" Kirsten asked.

"I don't smell anything," Angela said, but pulled back the blinds in the empty, dusty living room and opened a window.

The air that came in did nothing to ease the confusion.

"Let's go to the attic," Angela said.

"No," Kirsten said and stood on unsteady legs, leaning against the wall.

"The basement, then." Angela said.

Stephanie took a stand. "Not on your life. I'll never step foot in that basement again."

"We need to find Jake," Lois said.

"Which Jake?" Angela asked.

"Doesn't matter," Lois said. "I have a feeling that if we find one, we'll find them all."

The four women held hands and moved slowly into the living room. The sky darkened and a sour breeze moved through the window.

The house had been vacant a long time. All the lighting fixtures were gone, leaving bare wires dangling. In places, the carpeting had been pulled up, leaving scraps of mildewed foam pad. The walls were dingy and scuffed, the wallpaper torn. In the kitchen, the vinyl floor was cracked and broken, the sink missing, cabinet doors were splintered. Weird light filtered in from around a boarded-up window.

"Jesus," Angela said. "This looks like a horror movie set."

"I hear running water," Stephanie said. "Listen."

"I don't hear anything," Lois said, but they all bunched closer together as they contemplated their next move. "Parents' room next," Lois said. Huddled together, they left the kitchen and entered the master bedroom. Nothing but an empty room with purple flocked wallpaper.

"Now *I'm* going to gag," Angela said, touching the wallpaper. "Come on, you guys. Bite the bullet. Let's hit the upstairs and grab Jake, the ghost, or whoever he is, in the attic."

"You don't hear that running water?" Stephanie asked. "Sounds like it's running in the walls."

"The water's not turned on," Lois said.

"That stink," Kirsten said and squinted up her face. "It's going to get in my clothes."

Lois and Angela traded a look, then Angela handed over the flask and Lois gratefully gulped down half of the harsh booze. Fear flushed through her as dusk took a solid turn toward twilight.

Then Angela jumped, fell to a crouch and looked behind her, eyes wide with fear.

"Jesus Christ," Angela said. "Did you hear that?"

"No," Lois said.

"Like a truck full of bowling balls being unloaded." She looked at the ceiling. "Up there."

"My room," Lois said.

"Jake's room," Angela, Stephanie and Kirsten all said together.

"It's getting dark," Angela said. "Let's come back tomorrow. There's a nice lounge in the Holiday Inn, it's only about twenty miles…"

"No," Lois said, then grabbed them and pulled them all together. "Hey, Jake," she called. "We're here. What do you want?" She heard only tense, expectant silence as shadows deepened and heart rates increased.

Then her cell phone rang, and everybody jumped.

"Don't answer it," said Kirsten, her baby blues wide. "It's him."

Lois dug the phone from her bag.

"Don't!" Kirsten said. "Please don't. I killed him. When he was a baby, I held his nose and mouth shut until he stopped crying. I didn't mean to kill him, but once he was dead, I threw him in the garbage and told my parents he'd disappeared, you know, like kids sometimes do up here."

The phone rang again.

"I'm sorry," she sobbed. "I was just a little girl…"

The phone rang again.

"I'm sure it's just my office," Lois said.

"No, don't answer it," said Stephanie. "I swear it was an accident. In the bath. I didn't mean for him to drown, it just…happened. Oh God, Jake, I'm so sorry."

The phone rang again.

"Well, I crushed his goddamn skull with a hammer," said Angela, "and I was no kid." She drained her flask. "Answer it, Lois, I'll talk to him."

"My baby brother," Lois said, horrified with the confessions. "He died of meningitis when he was only five. I loved him so much."

The phone fell quiet and four aching women stood together in the shadows of an old, empty house.

"The water stopped running," Stephanie said.

"The stink's gone," said Kirsten.

"Four times he came into this house?" Stephanie asked. "*Four times?*"

"Looking for Lois," Angela said, "and her family. Looking for that love again."

"And finding only...oh, how sad," Kirsten said. "But he was always named Jake? Don't you think that's kind of weird?"

"Seems as though children bring their own names," Lois said.

"So what now?" Kirsten asked, her voice thready.

To Lois, the answer was obvious. "I'm too old," she said. "My children are grown..." she looked at Kirsten, still so young. "But you..."

"*Me?*" Kirsten said. "Why me? I'm not even married."

"Don't need to be married," Angela said. "Jeez. Just get pregnant in this house."

"You owe him," Lois said. "All three of you."

"It's true," Angela said. "We all did poorly by him, the little snot."

Kirsten commanded a stretched-out moment of silence while the other women looked at her and she looked at her options.

"Will you all be his aunties?" Kirsten asked.

Stephanie and Angela and Lois all nodded.

"And help a lot?"

They all nodded again.

"And be *nice* to him?"

"Okay," she said. "I wonder if Tommy Stonehocker still lives here. I had such a crush on him in sixth grade." She blushed. "I always thought we'd make gorgeous babies together."

"I'll call him," Lois said. "Bet he'll have no trouble cooperating."

"Then it's settled," Stephanie said.

"But first, we have someone else to call," Lois said. She picked up her cell and punched the last number redial to tell Jake the good news.

Memories from Home

Adam Moffatt sat in the sterile fertility clinic waiting room, trying not to make eye contact with the three pregnant women sitting in the other chairs. Well-thumbed magazines were all *Working Women*, or *Mothering* with a couple of small, outdated copies of *Prevention* stuck in the corner. He wished he had brought a newspaper with him. Only two other people waited in the little room, they looked like a normal couple. A normal, infertile couple, just like him and Rachel.

Adam sighed. Rachel had already been through her fertility tests, now it was his turn. Certainly, his test would be much simpler than her whole battery of tests. He shouldn't complain.

"Hey," the man said, then hauled himself out of the chair and approached Adam. He held out his hand. "You look like a local. Do you live here?"

Adam shook the man's hand and nodded.

"I'm Bob. Bob Matthews, and that's my wife Jeanette. We just moved to Sedona not too long ago."

"Welcome," Adam said, wishing he had a newspaper.

Bob sat in the chair next to Adam and said, "Say, do you know much about the rocks around here?"

"Not much," Adam said. "Rocks are not my thing."

"Not mine, either," Bob said, "but you sure have some beauties around here."

Adam nodded. The red rocks of Sedona were world renown.

"Yesterday, Jeanette and I went for a little hike, and we found a really unusual rock."

"Oh?" Neither Bob nor Jeanette looked much like the hiking type.

"Would you mind taking a look at it? Maybe you know what it is."

Adam shrugged. A rock was a rock.

"Honey?"

Jeanette opened her purse, walked over and handed Adam what looked like a chestnut. Brown, about the size of a slightly-flattened golf ball, but when she put it in his hand, it was so heavy that his hand hit his knee.

"Strange," Adam said.

"That's what we thought, didn't we, honey?"

"Very odd," Jeanette agreed, then went back to her seat, her purse held protectively on her lap.

Adam turned the rock over and over in his hand. It was warm, not cold as he expected. He held it up to the light, and for a moment, thought he saw an intricate web of veins and arteries through a transparent skin, but a moment later, that illusion flashed away in the glare of the florescent lights.

"I think it's something petrified," Bob said, then stood up and went to sit by his wife. "Maybe a dinosaur egg or something."

"Mr. and Mrs. Matthews?" A nurse in blue scrubs held the door open. Bob and Jeanette both stood.

"Here," Adam held out the strange rock to them.

"Keep it," Bob said, then followed his wife through the door to the examination rooms.

Adam turned the rock over and over, examining it from several angles. He could take it back to his veterinary clinic and x-ray it. Or he could just toss it into the bushes next to the parking lot. But he knew he'd keep it. People were always finding weird things in the hills around Sedona; maybe this would be some kind of a scientific discovery. An archeological find.

Back at the office he had an emergency gastric dilatation surgery to save a neighbor's cattle dog, and while he had the operating room up and running, he performed three routine feline spays. By that time it was mid-afternoon, and he still had to run all the way out to the Olson's ranch and see to their horse that had foundered, and to check on a goat that he suspected was carrying triplets, then to the auction yard to do a quick health check on all the animals before tomorrow morning's auction. He forgot all about the weird rock on his desk until he turned off the light in his office, always the last one to leave, and for a moment, it appeared as though the rock glowed with its own internal luminescence. But that was probably just a flash of reflection onto his exhausted retinas. Still, he put the heavy thing in his pocket and headed home. Maybe Rachel would be interested. She may have even come across things like this as she had been hiking the red rock hills of Sedona most of her life.

He put it in her hand as they both undressed for bed.

"What's this?" she asked, holding the rock under the nightstand lamp and peering at it through her bifocals.

Adam shrugged. "Some guy in the doctor's waiting room gave it to me this morning. Said he found it hiking."

"Weird," Rachel said and set it on the nightstand. "How did all that go?"

"Simpler than what you went through. They'll call tomorrow with results. Hey, remind me to take that thing back to the office in the morning. I think I'm going to x-ray it."

"Really?" Rachel picked it up and looked at it again. "It's just a rock."

"Maybe." Adam fell into bed, quickly reviewed his busy schedule for the next day, and within moments, slid into the sweet relaxing float of sleep.

It was an adventure they were on, he told himself, but those were just words. The truth was, he was scared, so afraid and so homesick he wanted to die. Adventure was just a term, because they had no choice; they could never go home again. Home had been poisoned, ruined, completely destroyed. To go off on an adventure was the only possible life left.

It was so, so sad. The sadness filled him like a great weight in his belly, and he hoped that where they were going they would be able to have a good life, one where their children would be welcomed and respected and treated well. The great adventure was the great lie all the adults told the young ones in order to keep them in line through the long journey, and to be that deceitful compounded his misery. The children would never know the once-beautiful home they had to leave behind.

It was so sad, it was so very, very sad.

Adam woke up sobbing into his pillow, the heaviness of grief almost too much to bear. Rachel moaned in her sleep. He sat up, awareness slowly coming back to him, grateful that whatever it was had only been a dream. Once he got his bearings: his familiar bedroom, the security light from the barn shining through the blinds on the wall, his beautiful wife in bed next to him—he wiped his eyes with the hem of his t-shirt.

Rachel moaned as if in pain. "Honey?" He shook her arm. "Honey? It's all right, it's just a dream."

Her eyes opened, but they rolled around as if she could still see into a different dimension.

"Rachel!" He shook her harder. "Honey, come back to me."

Her eyes came into focus and locked onto his. "Oh," she said. "Oh!" She sat up and hugged him. "It was so sad," she said. "So unbearably sad." And she began to cry.

Adam held her tightly for a moment, then reached over to her nightstand and got them each a tissue. "I know," he said, "but it was just a dream."

"Didn't feel like a dream," Rachel hicced. "It was so real. So real, so sad. We couldn't ever go home again. I was so *homesick*."

"It's okay, honey." Adam stroked her hair, wondering how they could have shared such a strangely specific and emotional dream. He wanted to tell her that he'd had the same dream but was afraid she'd overreact. Maybe later.

In the morning, Adam got up first, brushed his teeth, and went to make the coffee. His eyes were puffy and the sadness still permeated him like a bad hangover. He leaned against the countertop, listening to the coffee pot sputter, when he felt Rachel's presence behind him.

"Look what happened to your rock," she said.

Still wearing her nightgown, she set what looked like a brown flower on the granite countertop. Its petals looked thick and leathery, and at the center, where the pistils and stamens should be, was what looked like a little nut, like a small filbert.

"Wow," he said. "Really?"

"What is this thing, Adam?"

"I have no idea, honey. I thought it was just a rock. The people who gave it to me said they thought it might be something—"

The nut exploded and tiny seeds flew all over the kitchen, sticking to Adam's face, neck and forearms.

Rachel screamed as they stuck to her chest and arms. "Get them off me!" she shouted, dancing around the kitchen, brushing at the little seeds. "Get them off!"

But they couldn't be scraped off, they couldn't be peeled off. "I'll go get a scalpel," he said.

"No," she said, still clawing at them, "no scalpels on my face."

Adam watched as the seeds on her face changed color, became the color of her flesh, and then seemed to melt right into her. "Look," he said, and held out his forearm that had a half dozen seeds stuck to it. They, too, turned color and melted.

"Oh my god, those things are inside us now!" Rachel brushed her hand across her chest. "They're gone. They're all gone!"

Adam came around the side of the counter and took his wife into his arms. "It'll be all right," he lied, barely able to contain his own panic. "I can't imagine that there is anything to worry about."

~ ~ ~

The brown spots showed up later that afternoon. Everywhere a seed had landed on Adam's neck, arms or hands, a brown spot appeared and began to grow. He canceled his appointments and went home to find Rachel curled up on the sofa, crying.

"Honey?"

"Look," she said, and opened the blanket she had wrapped around her. One dark brown lump had begun to form under the skin at the bottom of her throat. "It's some kind of cancer, Adam. We're going to die."

"We're not going to die," he said, "but I am going to biopsy these things." He fetched his medical bag from the Jeep, but before he could open it, Rachel took his arm and began to examine a large brown spot on his forearm. "It's like that rock," she said. "It's a seedpod. It's one of those things like you brought home last night."

He held his arm under the table lamp. She was right. Just beneath the skin he could see the network of veins and arteries forming on a small growth, just like the pod that he had put into her hand yesterday. "They're growing fast," he said. "Maybe this will all be over by tomorrow morning." He paused. "Whatever that means."

She looked at him with sad eyes. "I want to rip them out and stomp on them," she said, "but I don't want to hurt them."

Strangely, he knew exactly what she meant.

Through the evening and into the night, as the heavy pods ripened, they gently picked them from the thin blisters on Adam's skin and threw them into a large basket that Rachel kept for her forays to the farmer's market. By 4 a.m., they were all gone except for the one big lump on Rachel's chest. That one just kept growing.

"We have to sleep," Adam said.

"I don't want to," Rachel said. "I don't want their sadness."

"Stay up, then," he said, "but I am exhausted."

Free of all the pods except for the one that continued to grow, Adam and Rachel got into their bed and held each other close. "If I die before I wake..." Adam said.

"Shhh," Rachel put a cool finger on his lips. "We'll be fine."

Adam closed his eyes and the sadness overwhelmed him. Over and over he heard himself saying, "I became a vet to help people, to help animals. There must be something I can do. *Should* do. *Will* do." But the task was overwhelming; there was nothing anyone could do.

The sadness consumed him.

He awoke to Rachel shaking him. Instantly alert, yet still swimming in the heartbreaking misery, he looked into her clear eyes and said, "What?"

She knelt on the bed and wiped the tears from his face with her soft fingertips. "This," she said.

A thin membrane of translucent skin hung limp and empty at the base of her throat where the object she held in her cupped hands had grown to baseball size.

Adam sat up.

"What is it?" he asked.

"An egg," she said. "I think it's an egg." She had a hopeful, bright-eyed look that he hadn't seen in a long time, not since the last time she was a week late with her period. "We can help them," she said.

"Honey," Adam tried to clear his head from the tendrils of despair that clung to his emotions. "We don't know—"

"I do. I do know, Adam. They need us. We can help them." She held out the round brown thing and opened his hand. She placed it there with reverence. "We don't have to do anything but let them hatch."

"Then what?" he asked.

"I'm not sure," she said, "but I know it's a good thing."

Adam hefted the egg. He wanted to latch onto Rachel's hope. She'd wanted to be a mother so badly, he couldn't deny her this, as weird as it was. He nodded. "Okay," he said. He cocked his head toward the basket of pods that had come from his skin, still sitting on the nightstand. Seed pods from him, egg from her. "What about those?"

Rachel smiled.

~ ~ ~

Tammy Fletcher sat fidgeting in the waiting room of the Flagstaff Fertility Clinic. There were at least a million things she would rather do than start a series of hormone shots, but that's what it had come to.

She looked up as a well-dressed man and his beautiful wife walked through the doors, spoke for a moment with the nurse at the desk, then sat across from her in the little waiting room. "Hey," the man said. "My name's Adam Moffatt and this is my wife, Rachel. You look like a local. Do you know anything about the rocks around here?"

My Brother and Me

I have a brother. At least I'm pretty sure he's my brother, although I don't remember having ever met him, or spoken to him, and my parents have never mentioned him to me, though I asked for a brother or sister probably a million times when I was younger. They never mentioned him.

The first time I saw him, a couple of years ago, he was standing in the middle of the back yard, in the moonlight, just standing there, looking at the house. I thought it was just one of the creepy neighborhood kids, so I went to the bathroom, and then back to bed, not giving it a lot of thought.

But the next time I saw him, he was in the living room, eating leftover lasagna. I knew it was the lasagna, because I saw Mom put it in that plastic container with the red top after dinner. He just sat quietly eating, and I watched him from the doorway. He didn't see me, well I don't think he did, at least not then. When he finished, he quietly put his dishes in the sink and went downstairs into the basement.

In the morning, of course Mom always gets up first, so she must be doing his dishes and putting them away, and nobody else knew that he was eating our leftovers.

And then I started to notice that she put after dinner leftovers in the fridge in such a way that they were clearly earmarked for him. So she knew.

But where he went after he went downstairs was a total mystery. There was nobody down there, and I knew the basement better than I knew my own room. There were no trap doors, no hidey holes, no places that he could be that I would not find him. He was not in the basement during the day.

Unless he was that spider in the corner.

Was he a spider in the corner during the day?

And why didn't my parents talk about him? Why wouldn't they tell me about this guy who came into our house at night?

My life became wrapped up in solving the mystery.

I got out of bed in the middle of the night every night, and I found him. He was somewhere in the house, doing something. Every night he came up from the basement and wandered around, doing this and that, never making any noise, never turning on a light, and then before dawn, he would go back down there.

I watched. Quietly, I watched him.

When the parents left me alone in the house, which they did now and then, about the time I turned twelve, I began going through their things. Somewhere, I was convinced, there would be evidence. How could my mother, who cooked for him every single day, not have some kind of indication of another man in this house?

How could they not talk about him to me?

Then one night I woke up to see him standing outside, his face against my bedroom window, staring in at me. It was the face of my nightmares, nightmares I'd had since I was a small child. That was the face, and what's worse is that now I knew that he knew that I knew. He smiled at me, but his teeth weren't right, and his eyes weren't right, and maybe it was a good thing that my folks hid him in the basement and only let him come out at night. I was horrified that he knew about me, and was afraid that he would torment me now, just because he could.

But this type of torment would be of a whole new level.

I turned away from him and pulled the covers over my head, but that didn't help. He knew about me. When I knew about him, *I* had the power, but now, his knowing about me somehow gave *him* all the power.

My stomach hurt and I had to pee and I thought I might throw up all at the same time. Instead, I just wrapped myself up in my comforter and swore I would never look out that window in the night ever again. Not ever again.

But that wouldn't help, because he was usually inside the house, and that meant he could easily just come into my bedroom.

I thought maybe I would never sleep again.

But in the morning, the sun shone, and the world seemed normal, and my night just seemed to be a distant nightmare.

Regardless, I did not stop my quest for information, and in the way my classmates hid their girlie magazines, I found a photo album wedged between

113

the mattresses of my parents' bed. I took great care to return the bedding the way it was, and then too nervous to look at it, I hid it between the mattresses of my own bed.

And that's when he began to torment me.

I would wake up at night and he would be towering over me, his contorted, grimacing face staring down into mine. I would stifle a shriek and pull the covers up over my face. One time, on my way to the bathroom, he was blocking the hall, daring me to push him out of the way. I ran back to bed and held my water for the rest of the night, until I saw dawn creeping over the windowsill, and I could safely dash to the bathroom in vast relief.

Even though I only saw him at night, I thought about him all day long. Where was he? Inside the walls? Under the basement floor? Was there some kind of an exit from the basement that I couldn't find? Was he inside the couch down there? No, I looked. It is a normal couch, not hollowed out to be some kind of a coffin for my nighttime antagonist.

Eventually, I mustered enough bravery to look at the photo album. So the next time my parents left to visit some friends, I pulled the album out. I wanted to have enough time to give it a real look before dark.

And there he was. Birth certificate, baby photos and everything. His name was Emory. His first steps, his little one-toothed grin, his fifth birthday cake, a summer at the beach. Then my birth certificate when I followed ten years later, photos of him holding me, the two of us in the wading pool, at the amusement park, at his thirteenth birthday party.

The phantom, the horrible nightmare, was my older brother.

I had to close the album and give some thought to it all. This was why my mother cooked for him, but why did they never talk about him? As far as they knew, I knew nothing about him. And why was he only out at night, and lived in the—where did he live, anyway? Up in the basement rafters?

His thirteenth birthday party, where I was three and he had a chocolate cake and the candle numbers one and three lit on fire, were the last photographs in the album. Nothing else. Nothing but empty pages. No more photos of me, either, although eventually I would have started Little League, and played clarinet in the band, starred in the school play, had my own family days at the beach, but nothing. I don't ever remember my parents taking any pictures of me at all.

Maybe they had another photo album of me, starting after my brother's 13th birthday. But even as I thought it, I knew that they didn't. Whatever happened had spoiled parenthood for them, and they were seeing me to adulthood by rote and duty. Not that I lived without parental affection, but I can't help but wonder if whatever happened to my brother had soured them on the whole deal. This reinforced my decision to not ask my mother or my father anything about him.

I could take care of myself.

Or so I thought.

Every night I wrestled with the idea that I could confront him, or talk with him, or reason with him, or ask him questions, or something. Surely we could connect on some level, some familial level. Surely he remembered me as a baby and since he clearly loved me then, he could love me now. I would love to have a brother, and perhaps if I did it correctly, I could bring him out of the darkness into the light.

And then my mother said a chilling thing over breakfast. "What kind of a party would you like to have for your thirteenth birthday?"

Oatmeal turned to dust in my mouth. She had never asked me anything of the sort for any of my other birthdays, so why now? *Why my thirteenth?* Emory's story ended after his thirteenth birthday.

I choked and coughed and muttered something.

"Many cultures consider the thirteenth birthday to be the beginning of a new phase of your life," she continued. "Some say that you have become a man when you turn thirteen."

I nodded, looking at my hands, appetite gone.

"Worth celebrating, don't you think?"

I nodded. "I guess," I said.

"Definitely," my father said. "It's the beginning of a whole new life for you."

That was enough. "What exactly do you mean by that?" I asked him. "What exactly is going to be different about my life after I turn thirteen?"

They turned and looked at each other and smiled.

I thew my napkin on the table and went to my room, grabbed my backpack and slammed out the door, headed for school.

They were going to do something to me when I turned thirteen, like they did my older brother. They were going to turn me into a monster like him. How could they? Didn't they love him? Didn't they love me? How could they? Was I destined to live in the cobwebs of the basement and eat cold lasagna every night?

I cried all the way to school, then went into the restroom, splashed cold water on my face, and blew my nose. There was nothing I could do. I was just a kid. I couldn't stop time, and my birthday was just a few days away. I was as good as dead.

Nobody came to my birthday party. No one else was invited. It was just the three of us, me and my mom and dad, and there were no presents. There was a chocolate cake with half-burned candles of one and three that my parents lit and smiled at me as if I was somebody special. But I didn't feel special, and I was scared half to death about what I was going to be like when I woke up in the morning.

If I woke up in the morning.

The cake was really good, though, like no other chocolate cake I had ever tasted, and at mom's urging, I had a second piece.

"Your life will be different from now on," my father said, "and so will ours. As this is the celebration of your becoming an adult, it is also a celebration of the end of our parental duties."

It was after that that I began to feel a little weird. Maybe it was just my imagination since I didn't usually eat things like cake. I wanted to ask him what he meant about "the end of their parental duties", but I was a little dizzy and felt strangely weak and wanted nothing more than to go to my room and lie down.

"We love you, honey," my mother called after me.

Apparently, the transition takes a couple of days, because when I woke up on the floor of my room, the house was completely empty. My parents had moved out. I wandered around the house in the dark, not knowing what to do with myself, as my bedroom was as empty as all the other rooms.

But I had my brother. He wasn't scary at all. He began to teach me how to live in the dark, how to find food in the refrigerators of the neighbors, how to make myself undetectable when the realtor showed the house to potential buyers. And when we were alone, we played, and laughed, and talked. He had waited a long time for me.

At last, I had a brother.

One Third of it All

Burt saw a building appear through the wavy haze of heat.

It had to be a mirage. There were no buildings out here. He was still a day away from Red Rock, a day away from meeting up with his buddies, a day away from food and drink.

A day away from drink.

He paused the horse and took off his hat. The afternoon sun burned his scalp right through his thinning hair. He wiped his sleeve across his sweaty, greasy face, and settled the hat back in its customary place.

The building still wavered on the dusty horizon. It appeared to be about five miles to the west, and he needed to get to Red Rock, due south, by tomorrow noon.

But he could sure use a drink. The horse needed water, too. They'd been dry for a full day in this searing sun. Burt's mouth was so dry his tongue had swollen. His lips were cracked, and he had been hearing weird music and seeing things out of the corner of his eyes for hours. The horse began stumbling not long after sunrise, and Burt couldn't afford to imagine the possibility that she wouldn't make it all the way to Red Rock.

Five miles to that building wouldn't set him back so far that he couldn't regain the time if he rode hard, and he'd be able to, if they both were filled up with cool water from a good well, and maybe some food.

He squinted off into the distance. Sure enough, the building was still there, or at least its roof was; the bottom disappeared in a series of heat waves.

The horse made the decision. She just began moving in the direction of the building, and he didn't stop her.

The boys would wait for him. They goddamned well better wait for him.

One-third of that loot was his.

It wasn't a building, Burt saw as they approached, it was a whole town. Several buildings lined a full block of a dusty, abandoned main street.

The horse made her way to an old metal trough, but all that was in the bottom was a little rusty rainwater. Burt slipped off the horse and let the reins drop. She wouldn't be going anywhere, except to search for more water. She could search behind the buildings; he'd search inside them.

He staggered out into the center of the street. "Hello?" he called. "Anybody here? Anybody have any water?"

No answer. Even the echo that bounced from the façade of the bank sounded dry and thirsty. Strange, that everything was so quiet.

Burt found the saloon and walked through its swinging doors.

Bottles of booze lined the shelves behind the bar.

A poker game had been dealt and never played, uneven stacks of chips at the hands. A bottle of whiskey and a shot glass sat on the edge of the bar. Burt uncorked the bottle, poured himself a shot and threw it down his throat. It seared his cracked lips, burned his dry tongue, and stung all the way down his raw throat, but it didn't quench his growing thirst.

There must be a barrel of water somewhere nearby. He'd find it in a minute and take some to the horse. Meanwhile, he looked around.

"Hello?" he called up the stairs. All the doors to the rooms where the girls worked were closed, and he heard no answer. "Where is everybody?" he asked loudly. He poured himself another shot, drank it, then grabbed the bottle by its neck and walked outside into the street.

The whiskey warmed him, but it only exacerbated his thirst. He needed some water, and he needed it now.

His horse was down at the other end of town, standing on the boardwalk, her head inside the general store. She probably smelled water inside there.

Hell, *he* could smell water. It was here somewhere.

Something ran across the dust, just outside of his vision. A child, perhaps. When he turned to look, nothing was there.

Maybe a rat.

The horse, he saw, had walked all the way into the abandoned general store.

Burt detoured from the store and pushed though the open door to the empty bank building. Three metal teller cages sat empty; the door to the back room closed. He tried it. It was not locked. He entered and found a full drawer of money sitting out at each counter, exactly as it would be if the bank were open for business.

"Hee ya!" he yelled. There was more money here than his one-third share in Red Rock, and chances are, neither of those crooks would wait for him anyway. Joke was on them, he thought. He had more here than he could carry. He looked behind the teller cages and saw the bank president's desk, and behind it, the vault door was unlocked.

He walked back and peeked in.

Stacks of bills filled the shelves. On the floor were strongboxes from the Pinkerton company stagecoach lines. Burt had hit the mother lode, and he hadn't had to work his ass off to do it.

But before he could fill bags with money, he needed a drink. He put his lips to the bottle of whiskey, but the swallow gagged him as if he had just swallowed a bag of salt. He needed water. He needed a long drink of cool water.

The horse had probably already found water by now, and he needed to as well, or he'd soon be in trouble.

Burt walked unsteadily out of the bank, blinked in the hot sun. His eyes felt crusty, gritty. He adjusted his hat and began walking toward the general store.

It was farther than he thought. He walked unsteadily what seemed like a mile in boots that were too big for his dehydrated, shrunken feet, but the store got no closer. Once or twice, he stumbled to his knees, waking up as he hit the ground, not entirely understanding how he got there. But he saw the door to the general store, and he slowly and painfully climbed to his feet and lurched his way toward it.

His tongue no longer fit inside his mouth, and the third time he landed face-first, his tongue became coated with dust and a thick, syrupy, sour, whiskey-flavored saliva that he could not shake.

All he wanted was water. He needed water. He could see it flowing all around him like a river, but he couldn't touch it.

The horse nosed herself out of the general store and whinnied, fresh water flying from her lips. Burt felt the spray across his hands and face and reached for her leg. Maybe she would drag him to the source. He tried to get up, but his withered legs would not hold him.

He'd have to crawl.

He knew that inside the store was water. Lots and lots of fresh water. A waterfall. A pool full of clean, clear water.

The horse, renewed having drunk her fill, danced just out of his reach, and he saw more droplets splat in the dust in front of his face. He reached for them with his tongue but sucked up only dust. He pulled himself along, fingernails ripping on the rutted road, his loose boots on the ends of weak legs trying vainly to gain purchase on the dried mud of the street.

All the while, the sun beat down upon his back, but no cooling sweat oozed from his pores. He had no juice left in him.

"Please," he said, or tried to say, but his tongue was in the way of his lips.

Something moved on the edge of his peripheral vision. For a moment, he thought he saw a dozen pair of boots.

With eyes watching—he didn't know or care whose they were—Burt clawed his way to the wooden steps of the general store, and crawled up them, step by painful step, dragging himself across the splinters toward the door. Inside was cool water. He knew it. It had to be there. The horse had found it.

He was so close. He could smell it. It smelled like a rainforest. It smelled like green grass and sweet, juicy pears. He could taste it. He could feel its breath upon his face.

He pulled his way through the door.

"Welcome to Grantsville," he heard a voice say.

Grantsville. He knew that name, Grantsville.

"Water," he tried to say, but it came out his lips as a moan.

"There's no water here, mister," someone else said. "No water for you."

There had to be water. He'd seen it on his horse's mouth. He could smell it. "Please," he tried to say, and crawled another few inches.

His hand landed on leather. Boot leather. Burt pulled himself along to plead with the man, but when he got face to face with the person who lay on the floor, he saw that it was Floyd, one of his partners. Floyd didn't look so good. His black tongue protruded between cracked lips, his face sunburned to blisters. Pus leaked out of one dead eye and pooled on the wooden floor. Floyd's lips twitched.

With a final, desperate burst of energy, Burt pushed himself up and looked around. Little Eddie was lying on the other side of the big barrel in the middle of the room. Once in a while he coughed and twitched, his boots scraping on the wooden floor in a little syncopated pattern. Around the back side of that big barrel were twelve men, sitting on stools, each with a tall glass of water so cold that the condensation ran down the sides and dripped onto the floor.

Floyd and Little Eddie never made it to Red Rock, either. They'd been rerouted, too.

"Water," Burt said to the men. They looked like charitable gentlemen, surely they would give him a drink.

"Hello, Burt," one of the men said.

Burt knew that voice. He squinted up through raw, crusted eyeballs at a towering man with a black hat. Sheriff King. He'd spent his share of time enjoying the sheriff's fine jail cell. But now the sheriff was a little translucent, and he flickered in and out of Burt's vision.

"Water," Burt said.

The sheriff leaned over and dribbled a little water from his glass onto Burt's head. With the last of his strength, Burt flipped over onto his back, hoping to catch a drop or two in his mouth, but the sheriff just laughed and sat back on his stool. "So you're asking for a benevolent gesture, are you?" All the men laughed.

"Please."

"Please," the men taunted him. "Please," They laughed and drank their water, letting it dribble down their chins and wet the front of their shirts.

"Welcome to Grantsville," one of them said again, and laughed.

Grantsville. Grantsville. Was that the name of the place that the stream had run through? In two weeks of back-breaking work, he and Floyd and Little Eddie rerouted that stream up in the foothills and sold the water rights to the fat cats down in Red Rock.

"We would have paid you double," Sheriff King said, "to put your shovels down, but you didn't even ask us."

"Instead, you poisoned our wells," one of the other men said.

The door to the general store opened again and dozens of vague people crowded in, shoes scuffling all around him. There were too many townspeople to fit; but they all crowded in, some had to partially squeeze inside others.

"Alkali is what trickled down instead of water," Sheriff King said. "Poisoned the children first, then the cattle, then the horses. You poisoned us all."

"All in one day," a woman's voice said. "We all died in one day."

"Just like you and your friends," the sheriff said. "All dead in one day."

"Soon now," someone else said.

Soon now.

He saw one of the women dip a cup into that barrel and bring it up full with water. She raised it high and poured it slowly back into the barrel.

The sound of it was the most beautiful music he had ever heard. Sweet, delicious, life-saving water. The barrel was full of it. Inches away.

He crawled forward, got his hands underneath him and raised up to his knees. He looked around at the crowd of dispassionate faces. He was sorry he'd caused them harm. Very sorry. He'd make it right. He'd make it good. He'd be happy to poison everybody in Red Rock if that would make them happy. He just needed a drink first.

He reached up and got his fingers around the lip of the barrel.

Water. He could feel it on tips of his fingers.

He pulled with all his strength, but he could neither pull the barrel over nor pull himself up to drink out of it.

"Please," he said, and everybody laughed.

"All in one day," someone else said, and Burt collapsed back onto the floor.

"Please," he said, but this time he was asking for death. Kill me now, please. Bash my head in, shoot me. Anything but this infernal thirst.

"'Course one day can last a long time here in Grantsville," the sheriff added, and everybody laughed. "Especially now."

Burt sagged back inside his bones, and tried to close his eyes, but they were too dry. He stared up at the dust swirling in the sunbeams and waited.

A Problem at the Pentagon

Dr. Rex Schiller couldn't remember the last time he gave a single thought to the military. Not in his lifetime had hometown boys been drafted and killed in faraway wars; he'd never seen a raucous protest and flag-burning on the steps of the local municipal buildings; never heard heart-ripping stories of flag-draped coffins and 21-gun salutes in Arlington. Those who died waging war or keeping peace—or whatever other mischief the National Defense Agencies deemed appropriate—were never missed. The military was a non-entity to the population after the Pentagon began breeding their own. Word of conflict on foreign shores barely rated mention on the nightly news. It was never the topic of discussion, at least not in his elite, professional circles, because it never touched him or his family. The United States lived within a cozy cocoon of denial, because the military liked it that way, and so did the citizens. The Pentagon bred their own, so it was no threat, and therefore not of interest to Rex and his neighbors.

Now and then a news item did break through, and Rex was always stunned to discover what a savage society existed outside the protected borders of the United States. Within the liberated, prosperous, separatist boundaries, Rex and his fellow Americans had become a society of philosopher-entrepreneurs, and they gave no thought at all to that which kept them safe.

Rex felt at times that the country was like a terrarium, safe and peaceful, while savages ravaged the world outside the not-so-transparent walls. Rex didn't mind. He kept busy at the lab with a rewarding career, his lovely wife and two magnificent daughters. He didn't shake anything up. He didn't need to. Life was good.

On a beige day like any other, an aide came into his laboratory bearing a business card with the Department of Defense seal and said that two colonels waited to see him. Rex was mildly surprised. He quickly put on a clean lab coat and met them in the conference room.

One of them slid a petri dish across the polished table in greeting. "Kill that," he said.

"What is it?"

"A virus."

"Obviously," he said. They wouldn't be bringing anything but a virus to a virologist. "What does it do?"

"Can you kill it?"

"I don't know. What is it doing? What have you tried? How prevalent is the infestation?" Rex looked again at the petri dish but saw nothing save a tiny discoloration in the center. "Can I have a larger sample? Perhaps a working sample—virus cells working on host tissue?" He was bored with his current project. It had stalled, funding was drying up, his job had become increasingly political and less scientific. He was ready for a new challenge and felt his heart rate increase at the prospect of this one.

The two military men looked at each other, and Rex noticed that they had an odd appearance to them. Their skin appeared slightly molded, too smooth; a touch waxy. Their noses were slight mounds, their mouths without lips.

So these are *created* soldiers, Rex realized with a jolt. He had never seen one in person before. Born and bred for battle. For the first time he wished he had chosen psychology as his scientific discipline instead of virology. He would have enjoyed interviewing them.

"You're to come with us," one said. "Your country needs you."

~ ~ ~

They took him home long enough to pack a small bag and kiss his wife goodbye. Hours later, they landed on the Pentagon helipad and Rex was hustled unceremoniously through a side door, down a corridor and then down a series of steps in a stairwell that looked like it was headed for the cellar.

A series of guards, all with that same bland look to them, facial features smooth and indistinct, opened a series of glass doors with electronic keycards. The next security level required a fingerprint scan and finally, way down deep in the earth, heavy metal doors opened only with optical scan. Rex's retina was processed under the authority of his escorts, and they were in.

Rex smelled it immediately.

Gangrene. It was one of those odors that a person never forgot. Rex had smelled it more than once in medical school, and this place reeked. He suppressed a gag.

All corridor floors, walls, and ceiling were lined with immaculate white tile. Small dark-haired people in blue jumpsuits scurried everywhere, cleaning. There were many military uniforms about, most of them wearing officer insignia like his escorts, but there were a few enlisted types, and many, many more of the small blue jumpsuits. They were cleaning, or delivering mail, or running errands of some sort. The military hierarchy in its full regalia.

The corridors were wide and tall, and sound echoed alarmingly, yet it was relatively quiet. Everyone went about their work with a quiet desperation.

So would I, Rex thought, if I had to smell death with every breath.

After what seemed like miles of tiled corridor, they went through swinging stainless steel doors and he was shown into a small, tidy, carpeted room with a bed, desk and bathroom. He stowed his suitcase in the closet while the escorts waited, then they continued.

But not far. They donned sterile gowns, booties, head wraps and masks, then went into an airlock.

When the doors opened on the other side, the stench almost knocked him down.

The colonels noticed his reaction.

"That's what the virus does," one of them said. "It's rotting the colonies."

"Don't worry," the other one said at his look of alarm. "It won't touch you."

"Jesus God," Rex said, holding a hand over his mouth, trying not to gag. "How can you stand that smell?"

"Our olfactory organs are tuned to detect chemical and biological warfare," the first one said.

Of course, Rex thought. They were soldiers—they would be concerned with the business of war, not the decomposition of their young.

Rex found it easier to breathe after a few minutes, as his sense of smell adjusted.

The floors, ceilings and walls in this part of the complex were all stainless steel, glinting in the indistinct light. Still the blue jumpsuits cleaned. Everybody going in and out wore the same type of surgical scrubs.

Rex was walked to a vaulted door with a window of thick glass. "This is the last disease-free colony," one colonel said. "If it becomes infected, we have lost the entire program."

Rex shouldered past them and looked through the window.

A vast warehouse-sized room contained a series of bluish-gray honeycombs of enormous proportion. Jumpsuited workers drove back and forth in tiny electric golf carts and deftly climbed about an immense network of scaffolding.

"As it is," the colonel went on, "officers and enlisted are crowded into this one barracks." Rex found his distaste amusing. Even here, the old separation of labor and management.

As they watched, a golf cart came down the row pulling a stretcher. It stopped in front of a cell not too far from the window.

"Fortunate timing," one of the colonels said. "A birth."

They watched as the workers broke what looked like a gel seal around the honeycomb cell and gently pulled out the pale, naked, glistening body of a man. They swabbed his face, wrapped him in sheets and blankets, put an oxygen mask on him, then the driver got back into his cart and pulled the stretcher away.

A swarm of little jumpsuits converged on the cell, cleaning it out, readying it for the next occupant.

Within moments, another golf cart drove up, a rack of what looked like stainless steel thermoses in the back. He stood by until the cleaning was complete, then he removed a thermos, twisted off the top and put something long and white inside the empty honeycomb cell. Then he went on his way, delivering larvae, while the jumpsuits cemented over the end with a substance they excreted from their mouths.

The whole process had taken less than five minutes. It was clearly production-line procreation.

Rex felt vaguely sick to his stomach.

The colonels noticed his discomfort and smiled at each other.

Then he took a deep swallow and took another look. There was something odd about the honeycombs. The row he could see was about thirty cells high and maybe five hundred long, but they fit together in a strange way, not like...

Oh. They were five-sided, not six.

Of course.

Pentagons.

He got a chill. This program had been going on far longer than any

American knew.

"Ready?" an escort asked. He nodded dumbly, and they continued down the stainless steel corridor.

"Here you have virus on...host tissue," one colonel said, and Rex looked through the window on this vault door and felt the blood drain from his head.

The honeycombs were black, furry and melting. Whole sections had slumped; semi-formed humans had tried to crawl out and hung halfway out of their cells. Some made it all the way to the floor before being overcome. Their bodies were sunken, and the darkness was growing on them.

Here and there: movement.

Nauseated and light-headed, Rex turned away.

"Officers..." one of the escorts said, and saluted.

～ ～ ～

Next stop was a briefing room, where Rex shook hands with his six scientific team members. Before he could become acquainted, the military treated them to the first of what would become a daily affair: a lecture on the importance of The Program, as they called it.

They were preaching to the converted, as far as Rex was concerned. He had heard stories of soldiers who came back from wars drug addicted or incurably psychotic. Breeding insect-people to do America's dirty work was fine with him.

But the task was a formidable one.

His initial hunch was to begin with the tough little virus that decimates beehives, but his colleagues had already exhausted that approach. Viruses are tricky because no two behave alike. There is one known virus that even spends a portion of its life cycle as a crystal. There are others that are genetically preprogrammed to mutate at random. Still others simply self-destruct. Rex wasn't the first virologist to be included on this research team.

But even as sophisticated as the laboratory equipment—and the military spared no expense—and as brilliant as the minds who were set upon this project, none of them had seen anything like it before.

Time was the enemy. The Pentagon knew infestation could break out in the final colony at any time. The pressure upon the team was enormous.

And they couldn't just spray the honeycombs with an anti-viral insecticide either, although they discussed that possibility in depth, both seriously and with tongue in cheek. They were careful about what they said to each other, as they knew that cameras and microphones were on at all times, but the pressure was so intense that now and then they had to laugh off the absurdity of the situation. Surely the military had psychologists who would understand. Nevertheless, Rex was always careful. He didn't want to be accused of treason because of a careless comment. He didn't know what to expect. He felt, for the first time, that he couldn't trust anything. He couldn't trust anything that he knew to be true. He could not imagine what he didn't know.

The problem, as the team discovered soon after Rex's arrival, lay in the DNA of the virus itself. It was unreadable. It confounded the computers—they continually spit out screens of irrelevant gobbledygook. It resisted any normal method of artificial replication for study. And the colonels were correct: it withered and died on any host except the larvae.

The virus destroyed the larvae and the organic honeycomb, by predigesting it all, cell by cell, reducing the mass to what could only be considered true primordial soup. New planets could be populated with life that would evolve from that liquid, were it to be planted in warm salt water under optimal conditions.

And then one day, Russell Allen, the bacterial specialist on the team, said it out loud: "This virus cannot be from this planet." And the team could ignore the fact no longer. They couldn't kill it because they couldn't determine its basis for life.

Russ was chosen to make this presentation to the colonels, but the whole team was called on the carpet. "We're out of options," Russ said, over and over, to waxen-faced, unsympathetic insectile faces. "The virus cannot be destroyed."

"Go back to work," was the command. "You will not go back to your families until the virus has been eradicated."

Rex and team went back to the laboratory, feeling like prisoners, not patriots.

～ ～ ～

After a period of shared, righteous anger, the team settled back down to work. They tackled the problem afresh like the professionals they were. While they were insulted by the circumstances, they were—to a man—intrigued by the challenge.

Their last option was to go at it from the opposite direction. Instead of trying to kill the virus, maybe they ought to make the larvae virus-resistant.

But this took even more time. They had to research records that went all the way back to the 1940s, when the larvae experiments first began. They had to study the controlled evolution of the species. And there were three major divisions: officers, enlisted, jumpsuited drones; and 347 minor ones. Each was differentiated in the larval stage by what it was fed.

And each day, the military dragged them away from the laboratory into the briefing room to pound away at them about the urgency of The Project.

Eventually—and time held little meaning for them in this subterranean environment—the seven scientists abandoned the laboratory altogether and spent days with pads and pencils in a conference room, trying to think up new questions to ask of each other, trying to find new avenues to probe.

They knew time was getting short. Any breach of integrity, a pinhole leak, and the last colony would become corrupted and die.

The days melded together, and one morning Steve Neems, the geneticist, whispered in Rex's ear: "They're fiddling with our clocks."

Rex nodded. He had long suspected that those responsible for The Program had rearranged the team's sleep hours until they were actually half hours, and work hours became hours-and-a-half. Ralph casually whispered in each team member's ear, and Rex watched as they each nodded in turn. The team was wearing down, and this was the reason. They had no time off, they had no exercise, no recreation. And now, they knew that the military had sabotaged their clocks. But knowing it didn't help any of them.

Creating a genetically resistant species of soldier was going to take an inordinate amount of time—too many generations of them for testing, too many potential viral mutations. It could possibly take generations of scientists. The team was grasping at straws.

And then Cliff Harris, the other virologist, hit upon the solution.

"Create an inoculation of the virus itself," he said. "A live vaccine, so to speak. An oral vaccine, like Salk's polio."

It was brilliant, and it was so conceptually basic that the whole team was amazed they hadn't hit upon the idea before. Perhaps other things besides the alteration of time was warping their thinking processes.

"Good idea," Steve Weems said loudly, so that anyone listening might hear. "If we weren't so goddamned tired, we could probably have figured that out months ago." Rex smiled at Steve, and they all nodded.

Regardless, all in an instant, they recognized that it would work.

"We'll have to get close to the larvae," Cliff said.

Everybody else fell silent.

"Very close."

"We'll have to get to the eggs," said Mitch Napolitano, the entomologist. "We'll have to see what lays those eggs, and what is fed to them."

"Going in and out of the incubator is impractical," Steve said.

Rex gave voice to the unthinkable. "We'll have to move our laboratory inside."

When they mentioned their plan to the uniformed leaders, they made immediate arrangements, and within hours, the team's housing facilities and laboratories were moved inside the one remaining disease-free incubator.

The best part of being inside the incubator was the end of the daily "patriotic duty" thumpings, though they still piped in the national anthem. Another advantage was the absence of the rotting stench. The air filters into the incubator were so fine they even filtered out smell.

The incubator was kept at a constant chilling fifty degrees, a major discomfort. It ran like a perfectly tuned machine, with no problems, no slipups, no paperwork snafus, no personality problems. The continual output of brand-new soldiers was astonishing and commendable.

From inside, the team discovered both the opportunity and its daunting barrier. Each larvae was fed a different solution, depending upon its specialty.

The jumpsuited drones, for example, were fed a particular mix of nutrients during their larval formation; the future pilots ate something else, the foot soldiers something else, the tank commanders something else, the boatswain's mates something altogether different. The Pentagon knew exactly how many of what kind of soldier, sailor, astronaut, or airman they needed, and they created exactly that, adjusting the mix as per their requirements. The team wasn't certain their every move was being monitored any more, and felt a freedom to laugh about the officers being fed royal jelly was refreshing as a day off.

So, the new task at hand was to create a live vaccine that could be administered to each of the formative creatures without altering their metamorphosis, yet making them immune to the decimating virus.

The difficulty was not in creating the vaccine, but in avoiding the creation of 347 different vaccines.

They got to work, eager to be finished with the distasteful business and get out of there. They had no idea what day it was, what month it was, but all were homesick and lonesome for their loved ones. They were motivated.

Each team member was assigned a drone as an aide, and the drones sat quietly, staring at the scientists in a most unnerving way. They began to send them on endless futile errands, until Ralph discovered that they were just as happy sitting in a row, facing the wall.

This was the stuff of the new military.

The team made swift progress, though trials were uncertain, and the failures were horrible to witness.

Eventually, the successes began to outnumber the failures.

The day came when the success criteria was met, and Cliff said the horrible words: "Let's feed this vaccine to the queen."

Everybody shuddered.

But it was the logical way. Just as a human mother passes immunity to her child while in its infancy, so the team only needed to protect these creatures until they were out of the larvae stage. As adults, they were immune. It was the perfect solution.

The team requested a meeting with the colonel. He took their trial data and conferred with his superiors. The word came down: the team could try the vaccine on *one* queen.

They readied the serum. They drew straws.

Rex drew the short one. He closed his eyes and said a short prayer while sympathetic colleagues breathed a sigh of relief and patted him on the back. This was the most distasteful of all tasks to date. But it had to be done. Someone had to do it. It was time to go home. Past time to go home, and Rex was afraid his wife would forget what he looked like. He made certain again, for the umpteenth time, that she was receiving a nice fat check for his trouble. Again, all team members were reassured that their families were being well cared for during their time of patriotic duty.

That phrase made them all want to gag.

A drone escorted Rex down an interminable hallway, his guts jangling. He didn't want to see this creature; he didn't even want to know of its existence. He agreed that there was a certain poetic justice to a created military, ought to be damned grateful, in fact, but the truth was, no matter how he tried to get over his revulsion, no matter how humanoid they appeared, these things were still insect people. Upon that, every member of his team agreed.

The incubator occupied square miles it seemed, and as they neared the queen's chambers, they passed gigantic row after row of honeycomb cells. "Which kind are these?" Rex asked the drone.

"Aggressors," he said.

Aggressors.

They walked another ten minutes in silence, while Rex thought about the military creating horrific worldwide problems in order to keep itself in budget and job security.

If this virus wiped out the American military, would world peace reign?

Or would the Pentagon return to the barbaric practice of drafting and murdering young men? Young human men?

Rex slowed his steps and pulled the serum from his pocket. It was a pale gray-blue, about the color of the honeycombs, about the color under his freezing cold fingernails.

What if, like the original primordial soup of life itself, this virus had been sent from the gods to *stop* worldwide aggression?

Another drone joined them, and now Rex had one on each side. It was clearly a forced escort. They picked up the pace.

Though they were already within a protected airlocked space, they went through another series of hydraulic glass doors to get to the queen's chambers. Drones scurried around her antechamber as if on methamphetamines.

Rex stopped. He needed to take a deep breath.

He didn't want to see the queen; he didn't have the stomach for it. Vague ideas of what she looked like flowed through his brain—some human female torso having her hair brushed and her nails filed while her enormous, pulsating, bloated white body shat one glistening white elongated egg after another? Where did this melding of human and insect technology come from, anyway, Roswell, New Mexico?

Atrocities were not new to the Pentagon. He had no appetite to view this one.

He slowed down; the escorts moved in closer.

He wanted to think this over; the escorts took his elbows.

No, he didn't want to see her. He didn't want to see her, and he didn't want to give her the serum.

He wanted this place to die.

With conviction he had never known, and courage he had never shown, he pulled away from them, turned around and ran, but the airlock doors were closed.

Bluesuited drones swarmed over him, knocking him to the ground, then pinned him down, sliming him with the binding excretion from their mouths.

They got the serum, and promptly forgot about him. Rex struggled against the sticky ligatures, and finally got loose.

Energized now, and solid in his certainty about the evil of this self-perpetuating program, he ran down the hall as if all the demons of hell were chasing him, which in fact, they could very well be. He was weakened by months of no exercise, by the cold, the lack of sleep, but he was on a mission.

He grabbed a steel chair and began breaking glass. Alarms began to shriek as he broke the glass into the chambers of the aggressors. He broke the glass into the chambers of the officers, the enlisted, the pilots, the sailors, the Marines, the special forces.

Drones swarmed around the damage, but he eluded them, pushing through their crowds like a linebacker headed for the goal line.

The goal line: A corrupted incubator. Any corrupted incubator.

This was an airborne virus. He knew all he needed was a hole to let it out and a hole for it to get in. It would take care of everything else by itself.

He smashed the window of the stainless steel door, slicing deep gashes in his hands and legs. He ran down the hall, yelling, screaming, trying to keep his flagging adrenaline up amid the mass confusion and the head-splitting alarms.

Then he was there. At the door to the death chambers.

Rex swung the chair, and glass fell as if in slow motion.

He fell down with the effort and sobbed, as the virus, along with the stench, burst forth.

Within moments, all the larvae would be dead.

And, he expected, so would he.

But the military had no such plans. Within days he was returned home to his family, and after a week, he went back to work at his job. He never communicated with any of the other scientists on his team; he assumed they either never left the Pentagon, refused his attempted communications, had completed their mission by vaccinating the rest of the queens, or all his attempts at communication were intercepted and nullified.

He haunted the cable news channels, but there was no word at all of bloody wars in foreign lands. No one else noticed. He startled awake in the night, smelling the stench of gangrene, then lay for hours, wondering who started the wars, who finished them, and who died, besides our manufactured soldiers. Was the Pentagon's purpose to eventually annihilate the world population, country by country? Was this the *new* ethnic cleansing? The New World Order? Were *we* the invaders, were *we* the parasites, feasting on the host tissue of cultures depleted and desolated by the wars that we started with our manufactured aggressors and then vanquished, much to the gratitude of the invaded country, by our manufactured soldiers? Is this how we maintained superiority for all these years? Through this incredible deception?

Eventually, he heard on the news, word of a skirmish. And then another, as the world outside the borders was made safe. Made safe again.

More and more Americans moved abroad, excited about finding brand new opportunities in newly benign countries.

Colonizing, it was called.

Playing Powerball

"Wretched excess." Davison Tollifer muttered to himself as he drove his battered Toyota up the long curving drive toward the family overindulgence of a house. The staff of gardeners kept the boxwoods trimmed within a millimeter; the rolling lawns sprouted not a weed; flowers bloomed on demand and faced the house with precision, their colors in perfect—and irritating—harmony. He knew that inside the mansion was just as perfect. No dust mote, cobweb, or blade of grass tracked in on someone's shoe would be on the marble floors for more than five minutes before a uniformed maid had it swept away.

Davison wished he had a memory of playing catch with his father on that lawn, or riding a tricycle around the circular drive, or picking flowers with his mother, but there were no such memories. He rode a horse instead of a bicycle. He played soccer at school. And flowers were delivered daily.

Nobody should have this much money, he thought.

And now, apparently, he was going to receive precisely one quarter of it: this estate in Pittsburgh, the Manhattan penthouse, the Tuscan villa, the stock portfolio, and who knows what else. He'd known the time was coming, of course, but now that it was here, he was appalled by the whole idea. What if Richard, Katherine and Peggy decided that *he* should have this horror of a house? What would he do then?

Turn it into the headquarters for Greenpeace? Give it to some other worthy cause? Sell it and donate the money?

Keep it?

No, never. He'd never keep it. He did just fine on his community college salary, teaching environmental studies, adding religiously to his 401k and living in his third-floor walkup apartment. He didn't want anybody in his world to know he came from this. Steel money. Evil money. The whole package had been a horrible embarrassment as he was growing up, and his feelings about it had never changed. He let his parents pay for his Yale education, then struck out on his own. He'd never taken another dime from them.

Unlike his siblings.

He pulled up next to Richard's Mercedes, and turned off the engine.

He checked himself in the rear-view mirror, ran his fingers through his hair, wished he'd taken the time to get a haircut, and grabbed the gym bag that was serving, this weekend, as his overnight luggage.

Despite the monumental waste that this estate represented to him, the mansion was situated perfectly in the peaceful countryside, just outside the reach of the steel mill stench. He took a moment to appreciate the quiet and the smell of the twilit air before approaching the front door. For a moment, he didn't know whether to ring the bell or just to open the door and go in.

Richard, a tumbler of their father's best scotch already in hand, opened the door with a smile that said it wasn't his first drink of the day.

"Dave!" He grabbed Davison in a hug that squished the breath out of him. "Good to see you, man."

Davison set his gym bag on the marble table in the center of the foyer. The house, never warm, echoed with silence. Twin curving staircases, inspired by Tara in *Gone with the Wind*, flanked the foyer. To the right was the library. To the left, the dining room. Straight ahead, the doors were open to what their mother always referred to as the salon.

A familiar feeling of melancholy and isolation settled over him as it always did whenever he came into this house.

"Kathy!" Richard called. "Dave's here."

Davison cringed at the use of his childhood name. "Davison," he said. "Please, Richard."

"Davison. Right. Sorry. Davison. And Katherine, not Kathy."

Richard, always larger than life, robust and barrel-chested, had a bit of a sunken air about him. At 51, Richard's face looked gray, except for his nose, which was covered with a starburst of red and purple veins. His hair was considerably whiter and thinner than the last time Davison had been home, and his normally taut stomach had relaxed into a bulging belly for the first time. While he didn't look very healthy, he was still the same bully he had always been.

"Hey," Richard said, looking through the windows to the circular driveway, "maybe you'll buy yourself a decent car now, eh? One you won't have to park on a hill?"

Before Davison could think of an answer, Katherine glided into the foyer, immaculate in crisp linen slacks and a silk blouse that matched the champagne in the glass she carried. Tall and pencil-thin, the very image of their graceful mother, Katherine seemed genuinely happy to see Davison, although the touch on his shoulders was light and she kissed the air near his cheeks instead of his flesh.

"You look good," Davison said. "As always."

"Thank you, darling, it's lovely to see you, too. Put your things upstairs and freshen up, then come join us in the salon."

"Is Peggy here?"

"We don't know where Peggy is," Richard said, the table steadying him against the effects of the scotch. "Seems she's given the staff some time off. Perhaps she's taking a little break herself."

"I'm sure she'll be back tonight," Katherine said, "since the funeral's tomorrow."

The funeral.

Davison nodded and grabbed his bag. "I'll be down in a minute." He took the south staircase steps two at a time and walked down the long hall to his old bedroom.

He hesitated at the door, his hand on the ornate lever. This room had been a guest room for him to sleep in since the day he was born. Nothing of a personalizing nature had been allowed, except on the shelves of his small bookcase, on his student desk, and pegged to the corkboard on the wall behind it. Everything else was placed just so by professional decorators and had to be maintained in its strictly defined position.

That had been Father's decree, and nothing would be different now.

He pushed the door open and entered. It looked exactly as it had last Christmas, and when he had returned home for his mother's funeral three months before that. The massive room was larger than his entire apartment in Charlotte, with floor-to-ceiling windows that looked out over the formal knot garden and reflecting pool on the south side of the house.

His mother had redecorated it right after he left for college.

That had been a shock the first time he came home to visit. He felt she wanted to erase his entire presence in the family's life. But then he realized it was *he* who wanted to do the erasing. Mother was merely redecorating.

That was when he stopped coming home. Only at Christmas was he here in body, but never in spirit. And even then, his presence was due to Katherine and the guilt she had long been able to induce in him.

Without thinking, Davison set his worn-out gym bag on the bed. Horrified at the inappropriateness of it—this unsightly thing lounging on the perfect bed like a malignancy—he moved it quickly to the floor.

But wait a minute, he thought. Nobody was here to reprimand him. This was *his* bed for the night, and he could put his tattered gym bag on it if he damn well wanted to. So he did. He unzipped it and took his toiletry kit to the bathroom.

Hell, the *bathroom* was bigger than his apartment in Charlotte.

He brushed his teeth, splashed cold water on his face, dried it with a scented towel that had apparently been dyed to match the accent tiles, and then went downstairs to see how long he had to stay here. He wanted to leave tomorrow right after the funeral and drive straight through, so he could be back in class on Monday.

But something told him that this wasn't going to happen.

In this family, nothing was ever that easy.

~ ~ ~

Davison found Richard sprawled out on the sofa in the living room. Silk. Chenille. That sofa would have cost Davison an entire month's salary, and there was Richard with his shoes on it, an empty scotch glass dangling from his hand.

"Think I'll move in here," Richard announced. "Let someone else take care of me for the rest of my life."

"Dad leave this place to you?" Davison asked, annoyed that Richard had information that he hadn't. He was even more annoyed that he had risen to the bait. He didn't *care* if Richard got the mansion. He only knew that he didn't want any part of it. The daily upkeep of this place could feed a small village in South Africa.

"Default position," Richard said. "I'd arm wrestle you for it, but I'd bet that Matisse over there that you don't want it, and Katherine would rather have the villa. So I might as well take it."

Davison went behind the bar. He poured himself a glass of tap water and added a couple of ice cubes from the bucket. "Where is Katherine?"

"Upstairs. She wanted to see the old man's bedroom. People are apparently coming tomorrow to take away all the hospital crap." Richard shivered. "Pretty goddamned ghoulish, if you ask me."

Davison perched on the edge of the suede ottoman, still a guest in this, his boyhood home. No, he corrected his thought. *Boyhood house.* This place was never his home. He took a moment to appreciate the sweeping view as the sunset colors in the sky faded and the lights of the city below began to come alive.

Richard stretched. "Might make some changes around here," he said. "This room needs a decent media system, or maybe I'll turn the library into a real theater—"

"Dad might have left the whole shootin' match to the ASPCA or something," Davison said.

Richard threw his head back and laughed too long, too hard, booze fueling his mirth. "ASPCA. They'd take one look at Dad's big game trophies and give the money back." He laughed again so hard he began to cough.

"Enough scotch for you," Katherine said as she soundlessly appeared at the doorway. She glided to the wing chair that matched the sofa and lightly sat. "Upstairs is ghastly. Ugh! I'm sorry he had to go through all that. Mother's sudden death was much... neater."

Neater? Davison thought. *Neater?* Even death had to be tidy in this house.

"I was just telling Dave here that I would take this house, and you the villa," Richard said.

"And that leaves?" Davison asked, then cursed himself for being interested.

"That leaves New York," Katherine said. "And the stocks."

"We'll have to divide up the stocks to pay for the upkeep on the places," Richard said.

"What about Peggy?" Davison asked. "Don't you think she'll have something to say about this? And what about Father himself, in his will?"

"Well, of course," Katherine said. "I believe the attorney is coming to the funeral and we will meet with him afterward."

"Peggy doesn't want any of this shit," Richard said. "We'll give her a million and she'll be happy."

"Whoa," Davison said getting up to refill his glass. "That's pretty harsh."

Richard shrugged. "So you'll take New York, eh?"

"I'm happy in Charlotte," Davison said, "doing what I'm doing."

Richard smiled at Katherine. "Then it's you and me, babe. A mill to Peggy and the rest divided two ways," he said.

"Now wait a minute," Davison said. "Let's not get ahead of ourselves here."

"Ignore him," Katherine said. "He's had too much to drink. Of *course* we'll abide by Father's wishes. And if he didn't leave anything concrete, then we'll work it out amongst ourselves. It will be fair."

"Fair schmair," Richard said, with a sudden burst of venom.

Davison leaned against the bar and sipped his water. Richard couldn't hurt him anymore, he reminded himself. The power of the bully had been equalized over the years. Still, Richard's bullying had the power to make his face flush and his heart race.

"You spat on everything Father accumulated during his life," Richard said to Davison. "You sneered and turned your nose up, and now you don't get to have it. Any of it. I'll fight you if you even try—"

Katherine stepped to the sofa and put a hand on Richard's shoulder to stop him. She took the empty glass from his hand and set it on an end table. "Nobody's going to fight, Richard. We'll see what tomorrow brings."

Richard scowled.

"When we're all sober," Katherine added with a knowing look at Davison.

"Good idea," Davison said, grateful to his big sister for always being the peacekeeper. They were all adults, and she still had to be the peacekeeper. That said a lot about the disturbing family dynamic. Eager for a change of pace, he asked, "What is there to eat?"

"I don't know," Katherine said. "Shall we raid the fridge?"

~ ~ ~

"Do you remember Alabama?" Katherine asked with a twinkle as she dipped the tips of her salad fork into a small dish of dressing.

Davison set down his tomato sandwich. "How could I forget Alabama? It was the only family vacation we ever took."

"Why the fuck did they take us all to Alabama?" Richard spoke around a mouthful of deli roast beef.

Mother would be horrified at Richard's table manners, Davison thought. She'd be aghast that they were eating in the servants' kitchen, too, but that was where they found the food. The regular kitchen was filled with cases of a canned prescription drink for their father's last meals, and little else.

They each fixed their meal and then sat on barstools at the granite breakfast bar to eat.

Davison used to eat here with his nanny when his parents weren't home.

It always made him feel a little bit naughty, and he enjoyed keeping the secret.

"Strange, wasn't it?" Katherine toyed with her dainty salad, but she didn't put a single lettuce leaf on her fork. "I went everywhere with Mother." She set her fork down and smiled. "Paris, London, Geneva, I remember she took me on a trip just to study art in Florence. That was a nice time. You took trips with her and with Father, too, didn't you? But for our only family vacation, all six of us together, we went to Alabama. Isn't that odd?"

"They were busy," Davison said. "Mother had her charities, and Father, well, you know. He worked. He always worked."

"He *always* worked," Richard said.

"The Redneck Riviera," Davison said, remembering his first time in the ocean. "It was a lot of fun being at the beach, though. I was about, what, eight?"

Richard sucked in a half cup of reheated coffee. The food in his stomach was having a positive effect on his disposition. "I was eleven," he said, "Kathy was ten, you were eight, and that made Peggy, what, six?"

"Dad must have had a business meeting there or something," Davison said. "I remember us being there, but I don't remember him being there."

"Typical," Katherine said.

Father was absent most of the time, Davison thought. The Bible thumpers in Charlotte rattle on about the love of money being the root of all evil. He heard it every time he turned on the television on a Sunday morning. But in Davison's experience, it was more like the *pursuit* of money to the exclusion of all else—especially family—to be the root of all evil. "Anyway, it's too bad we never did it again. Even here in Pennsylvania. Couldn't we have all gone camping or something?"

"Camping?" Richard and Katherine said in unison.

"Guess not," Davison said wryly. "Mother would never have gone camping. She might have wrinkled something silk."

"We could go now," Katherine said.

"Camping?" Richard asked, spreading butter on a slice of bread.

"God, no. But the four of us—none of us are married at the moment—we could go somewhere, have a vacation together, have some fun for once."

"That's a great idea," Richard said. "Where?"

"The Galapagos?" Davison offered.

Katherine wrinkled her nose. "That's nothing but bird poop and walruses. How about Dubai?"

"African Safari?" Richard tossed in. "They have some nice ones these days."

"Sydney? Rio? *World cruise?*" Katherine looked at Davison as if expecting him to react with his usual liberal disdain. "Money is no object, remember."

Money is no object, Davison thought. *Money is no object.*

Davison had colleagues who regularly went to Harrah's in Cherokee to gamble, but as intrigued as he was, he never had gone. His thrifty soul would not allow it, nor would he support the thugs who bankrolled the tribal casinos. "If money is no object," he said slowly, "then let's go spend a week in Monte Carlo."

"To gamble? Davison!" Katherine said in delighted surprise. "I would never expect that from you."

"I always thought if I won the lottery, I'd set aside a modest amount and try my hand at some poker. Or blackjack."

"About time you took a little risk," Richard said. "But the lottery? Do you buy lottery tickets?"

"My whole *life* is riskier than yours," Davison said. "*Much* riskier. And yes, occasionally I buy a lottery ticket."

"You're too much," Richard shook his head and laughed. "All this—" he waved his hand to take in the room and what lay beyond it—"and *you* buy lottery tickets. You kill me."

"Monte Carlo is a brilliant idea!" Katherine rerouted the conversation.

"Let's go this summer," Davison said, pleased that they had warmed to his suggestion. "I'm not teaching summer term this year." He dug a couple of olives out of a jar and passed it to Richard.

"Quit that dead-end job," Richard said. "You're a man of independent means now."

A man of independent means.

"Think Peggy would enjoy Monte Carlo?" Davison asked.

"Of course!" Katherine said. "What's not to love? We'll have a ball! It'll be the family vacation our parents should have taken us on all along, only more fun. There's sun and beach."

"And that damn casino," Richard said. "The last time I was there, they took too much of my money. I need to get it back."

"It's where millionaires go to meet other millionaires," Katherine said. "It might be good for all of us. We could jump start our pathetic love lives."

"Has Peggy ever been out of the country?" Davison asked. "I mean, apart from trips with our parents?"

"Peggy has never been anywhere," Richard said, "except in this house."

"Then it'll be our thank you gift to her," Katherine said. "Taking care of them couldn't have been easy for her."

"Hell, Mom went fast," Richard said, dismissing Katherine's concern. "And Peggy always had adequate staff." He stuffed the last of the roast beef into his mouth, let his fork clatter to the empty plate, and leaned forward, elbows on the countertop, chewing.

"Still," Katherine pushed her plate away, "you haven't seen his room upstairs. It was no picnic for Peggy."

"Hey," Richard said. "Growing up with them as parents wasn't a picnic, either. We all got out as soon as we could."

"Peggy didn't," Davison said. His appetite had disappeared at this turn of conversation. He had always felt guilty that Peggy had been the one to stay home, that she was the one left to care for their parents when they fell ill.

"Peggy made her choices," Richard said. "Just like you did."

Davison knew what Richard was talking about: his refusal to take a monthly stipend from their parents. Both Richard and Katherine had gladly lived off the generosity of their father, but Davison had chosen a different path. Richard never passed up an opportunity to jab at him about it, and Davison was just beginning to understand why. Richard was envious of Davison's independence.

"And I'm sure we're all happy with our choices," Katherine said. She picked up her champagne glass. "And thrilled with the way our lives have turned out." She drained the glass and set it, just a little too hard, on the granite tabletop.

"Things will be different from here on out." Richard hoisted his coffee cup. "Here's to the future," he said.

Davison clicked his water to Richard's cup, and Katherine offered up her empty champagne glass for the toast, then got up to refill it. Davison looked down at the mess they'd made on the kitchen table and all across the countertop. "Shall we clean this up?"

"Peggy'll be home soon," Katherine said. "Let's go back to the salon." She picked up her refreshed glass and glided from the kitchen.

Davison put his plate in the sink, then followed his sister. "Shouldn't Peggy be back by now?" He checked his watch. He'd been home for less than two hours, but it felt like two days.

Richard grabbed a handful of chocolates from a candy dish on the bar, then flopped again onto the sofa, his usual position. The sofa had been replaced often since their childhood days, but Richard's propensity for flopping on whatever was long enough to hold him had never shifted. "What are you really asking, Davy-boy?"

Katherine laughed, folded herself into the wing chair, tucked her feet underneath her. "What are we all really asking?"

Davison wasn't sure what they were talking about. He leaned against the fireplace and looked questioningly at Katherine, who laughed again. He knew if he closed his eyes he could believe it was his mother, sitting in that chair, laughing that tinkling laugh that Katherine had inherited.

"Oh, Davison," Katherine said. "You are so sweet. It's the *will*, darling. We all want to know what's in the *will*."

"Do you think Peggy knows?"

"Hard to say," Richard said, chewing a chocolate. "Probably. Maybe that's why she's not here. She doesn't want to lie to us by telling us that she doesn't know, and she doesn't want to spill the beans before the appointment with the attorney tomorrow."

"What I would like to know," Katherine said, "is why *you* don't know, Richard. Surely you've asked."

"I've asked," Richard said. "Of course I've asked, but the old man wouldn't tell me. 'None of your business, you vulture,' he said."

Davison carefully wiped the condensation from the side of his water glass, hoping he looked calmer than he felt. "He called you a vulture? I mean, Richard, he actually called you a vulture?"

Richard raised an eyebrow. "Yep," he said.

"I don't think he was in his right mind at the end," Katherine reasoned.

"He was in his right mind, all right. He was a bastard, and we all know it." Richard pulled himself up off the couch, dropped the handful of chocolates onto the coffee table and headed for the scotch decanter.

"How can you say that about him?" Davison felt his face growing hot. "He has supported you in a pretty fancy lifestyle all these years. You could use a little gratitude."

"Richard, darling." Katherine put her half-empty champagne glass on the side table. "Let's not drink."

"Yes, please," Davison said. "Alcohol has a way of... I don't know. Exacerbating emotions."

"Not for me," Richard said. "Whenever I'm in this house, I want to get numb, and this does the trick." As he tried to put the heavy crystal stopper back into the decanter, it slipped from his hand and smashed on the marble floor.

"Oops." He kicked the larger shards under the Italian Renaissance cassone, threw the scotch down his throat, and returned to the couch. Once again, he flopped. "As to gratitude—well, a bastard is a bastard, Davy, and money has nothing to do with it."

"He has been very generous with you," Davison said. "Both of you. And Peggy."

"And you," Katherine said.

"Yes, of course," Davison agreed. "He didn't have to be so generous with us."

"Yes, he did," Richard said. "He raised us to expect to live like this."

"No, Davison is right," Katherine said. "He didn't have to be so generous. I think Mother and Peggy convinced him to continue our allowances, Richard."

Richard rubbed his palms together. "How nice of them. And now we're about to get our hands on the whole enchilada."

"*If* he left it to us," Davison was tired of this conversation. He was tired of his drunken, greedy siblings. He was tired of this house, he was tired of his parents. He was tired of feeling guilty about not visiting them, tired of worrying over them as they grew older, tired of feeling horrible that he had moved so far away and left Peggy to take on everything that rightly should have been shared among all four of them.

He just wanted to be *done* with the funeral and get the fuck out of Pittsburgh. If he never heard the term "steel money" again, he'd be happy. "I hope he left it all to charity," he said.

"He wouldn't dare," Richard said. He sat up, his attention riveted on his younger brother's inconceivable suggestion.

"It is his money, Richard," Davison continued. "*He* made it, not *you*. Why do you think like you have a right to it?"

"Because it's our birthright," Richard said. "One quarter of the Tollifer estate belongs to me, and that's all there is to it. At *least* one quarter."

"Surely you've planned for your futures," Davison said, "put some money away after all these years." He looked at Richard, who looked blankly back. "Haven't you?"

Katherine barked out a laugh.

"I just don't get how you can feel entitled to all this—" Davison gestured around the expansive room "—this wretched excess."

"Wretched excess is our bare minimum, Davison," Katherine said. "You'll learn. You'll see how easy it is to become accustomed to nice things."

"No shit," Richard said. "Once you fly to Europe—or anywhere else, for that matter—in a Lear, you won't be too happy catching JetBlue."

"Oh, my god." Davison sat on the piano bench and ran his hands through his hair in frustration. "Father may not have been perfect, but he and Mother did a lot of good in the world. Especially mother, with her charities, and the foundation. We should be talking about *them* tonight. We should be talking about who they were and what they did for us, for the community, and for all the people they employed over the years. We should be a little grateful."

Richard stared into space.

Katherine picked at a cuticle.

"I think I'll go to bed," Davison said in resignation. "What time is the funeral?"

"Ten," Katherine said. "We meet with the attorney at one."

"Okay," Davison was eager to be finished with the entire mess. He thought he just might keep his mouth shut from now until he was on his way home again. There wasn't anything he could say that would make a difference to his siblings and he knew it.

As he stood up to go to bed, he took one last look around. He realized that this might be his last trip to this house. This weekend might be the last time he saw any of his siblings, too. They had nothing in common, and perhaps it was time to be rid of all of them all in one fell swoop.

The feeling made him uncommonly sad.

"Good night," he said.

"'Night," Katherine said.

Richard said nothing.

But as Davison got to the foyer, he heard a car door slam.

Peggy was home.

~ ~ ~

Davison helped her bring grocery sacks into the house. He was appalled at her appearance. Peggy looked pale and exhausted. Always tending toward pudgy, she was now obese, her hair straggly and an inch of gray showed at the roots. She wore black sweatpants and a man's shirt, and her complexion was marred by blotches and pimples. She hadn't looked like this last Christmas. Ten months with their dying father had taken a toll.

Yet once the grocery sacks were on the counters in the kitchen, she gave Davison one of her trademark, hard, heartfelt hugs.

"Before you say anything—" she looked pointedly at Richard and Katherine who stood in the doorway, "I have a new dress for the funeral and an appointment to have my hair done early tomorrow, so I won't embarrass either of you." Then, with a deep breath, she turned to the bags on the countertop. "I bought food." She looked at the mess they'd left. "But I see you've already eaten."

"Where's the staff?" Richard asked. "Why are *you* shopping for groceries?"

"Father gave them each fifty thousand dollars and a month off," Peggy said.

Katherine gasped.

"It was the right thing to do," Peggy went on. "They'll be back in October."

"Fat chance," Katherine said.

Davison wanted to slap Katherine. The wear on Peggy's face was more than obvious, and he was sick with guilt. The fact that his brother and sister felt nothing—the way they were treating Peggy like one of the servants—made his blood pressure rise. His heart pounded in his ears. Still, fifty thousand dollars. What he could do with fifty thousand dollars! Get his PhD for starters.

"Let's talk about Father's will," Peggy said.

"Will I need a drink?" Richard asked.

Peggy showed her familiar crooked smile. "It couldn't hurt."

Peggy pulled a bottle of iced tea from a grocery bag, and Davison got another glass of cold water from the refrigerator dispenser. Back in the salon, Richard went immediately to the scotch, and Katherine refreshed her champagne.

Richard didn't flop this time; it was as if he needed to be vertical to understand everything correctly. Katherine took up her perch in the wing chair, and Peggy relaxed in the big suede chair, where she kicked off her shoes and put her feet up on the ottoman. She opened her tea and drank half of it down. Davison regained his place on the piano bench, a strategic position where he could see everyone and hear everything.

"It's nice, isn't it? Us being together," Peggy said.

"It's good to see you," Davison said. "I'm sorry that you had to endure all this alone."

"It was hard," Peggy admitted. "Father fought that cancer to the end."

"When did he have presence of mind enough to give the staff such generous bonuses?" Richard asked.

"He was a generous man, as you have, no doubt, noticed. He was a good man, a brilliant man, and our staff understood that," Peggy said. "You have no idea what they did for us. Until we hired a full-time nursing staff, Martha and Klaus did everything. They did their jobs. Martha ran the household, Klaus took care of the property, and in addition they also took care of all Father's needs."

"Then what did you do?" Katherine asked while sipping her champagne. "Besides eat, I mean."

Peggy paused. She looked directly at Katherine. "You have no idea about anything." She spoke without rancor. Her self-control amazed Davison. He could never have responded so calmly.

"Shut up, Kathy," Davison said to her. "Just stop it, all right?"

Katherine raised her eyebrows and pursed her lips.

"So where have you been all day?" Richard asked Peggy.

Peggy fortified herself with another swig of her drink, set it down and began rubbing her swollen feet. "I had to have one of father's suits altered to fit him, so I picked that up and took it to the funeral home, went to the caterer's, the attorney's office, and then bought groceries," Peggy recited. "The caterer will be here early tomorrow to set up for the reception after the funeral."

Richard keyed in on the only words important to him. "You went to the attorney's office? Why? Don't we all have an appointment there tomorrow after the funeral?"

"We made that appointment in case you wanted to talk with him, but there is really no reason, as the estate is all settled."

"How can that be?" Katherine asked.

Peggy took a long drink of her tea, then looked briefly at each of her siblings. "Father left everything to me," she said.

"You mean the arrangements," Katherine said.

"I mean the estate," Peggy told her.

Richard relaxed against the couch, amazement on his face. "You're fucking kidding." He looked at Katherine.

Davison smiled. This went a *long* way toward assuaging his guilt. Peggy

148

deserved it all.

"I think we *will* go to that appointment tomorrow," Katherine said. "A man can do things at the end of his life when he's sick and not in his right mind."

"He was in his right mind," Peggy said. "The attorney will tell you that. There were physician certifications and witnesses, just to keep it incontestable. And he left provisions."

"Such as?" Richard prompted.

Such as the fifty thousand each to Martha, Klaus and Henrik."

"Henrik?" Richard said. "Who the fuck is Henrik?"

"The groundskeeper."

"And *he* gets *fifty thousand dollars*? Just like that?"

"Jesus God," Katherine said.

"Not only Henrik," Peggy told him, "Dad also left a nice gratuity to the people who manage the Italian property and the Manhattan property."

"How much of a gratuity?" Richard asked.

Peggy paused. She regarded Richard with exaggerated patience. Davison knew exactly how she felt. "I know that you have every right to this information," Peggy said, "but could you tone down the accusatory attitude? These were Father's wishes."

"Maybe," Katherine said, her eyes narrowing in suspicion as she regarded Peggy.

Davison watched Peggy gather her resolve around her. As if watching her father waste away wasn't horrendous enough, she still had two terrible events yet to endure. This was one of them, and the funeral was the other. But that would be the last. Peggy was strong, and she'd get through both, despite Richard and Katherine. After that, Davison realized, she deserved to do whatever she wanted with her life and her money.

Admiration for his baby sister flooded through him. He sipped his water and waited to hear what she had to say next, ready to come to her defense if Richard and Katherine got nasty with her. Peggy didn't deserve nasty from anybody, and he'd see to it that this conversation remained civil, no matter what it took. If his parents mentioned each of the staff in the will, then surely they mentioned him as well. For the first time, Davison found himself as interested in the details as his siblings.

"Whoever wishes they were," Richard said, "let's hear about these provisions."

Peggy took a deep breath. "As I said, the bulk of the estate was left to me to manage. I'll keep up the foundation and carry on Mother's philanthropy. You, Richard, and you, Katherine, will retain your allowances until your deaths."

"With the standard annual cost of living increases?" Katherine asked shrewdly.

A cloud of impatient disapproval crossed Peggy's face, but instead of saying what she was thinking, she politely said, "Of course."

"Well, I can live with that!" Katherine said. She held up her champagne glass. "To us, Richard!"

Richard raised his glass to her, then drained it of scotch.

Davison waited, but Peggy seemed to have nothing more to say.

"What about. . ." he hated the sound of the word he was about to say. "What about me?"

"You never wanted anything, Davison," Peggy said. "Father respected that. He admired it, actually. He assumed it would continue to hold true."

Davison was stunned to speechlessness. He was prepared for just about anything this weekend, but he was not prepared for this.

If there were ever an injustice in the world, this was it: Richard and Katherine assuming their stupid lifestyle while he continued to slave away at a wretched community college job.

In one quiet moment, Peggy had taken away his new car, his middle finger salute to the community college board of directors, his trip to Monte Carlo in a private Lear jet, his Ph.D., his life of leisure, his *everything*. She had pulled it all out from beneath him.

Oh. Wait.

This had to be a joke.

Katherine and Richard had put Peggy up to it, and they were waiting, in their twisted type of glee, for his reaction.

"Very funny," he said, managing a smile. "Joke's on me. You guys got me."

"It's no joke, Dave," Peggy said. "I'm sorry if you're disappointed. Father didn't want what happened with them—" she nodded toward Katherine and Richard— "to happen to you."

Disappointed? He looked over at Katherine, who was gazing at him with an amused expression. Richard, too, was smiling at him, watching his reaction. "Disappointed?" Davison asked. "That's what you think I am?

Disappointed?"

He had never wanted his father's money, but he had always wanted the option. He'd always said "no, thanks," because there had always been a string attached. Richard and Katherine had danced like puppets to their father's whims, but Davison? No. He'd chosen to take no money from his father as long as receiving the allowance had meant being at his father's beck and call.

But now, to be cut completely out of the will?

No. No way.

He was the one who was self-sufficient. *He* was the one who provided for himself, paid his taxes and added value to the community.

Hell, he was the one who *deserved* an inheritance.

He was the *only* one who did.

He set his water glass on the polished grand piano. He looked directly at Peggy. "No," he said. "It's my turn now."

As soon as the words were out of his mouth, he saw the truth in them. He stood up and faced Peggy, the courage of the righteous flowing through him. "*No.* It's my turn. It's my *goddamned* turn. One quarter of the Tollifer estate belongs to me, and that's all there is to it. At *least* one quarter. *I'll fight you for it.*"

He heard Katherine laughing behind him, and she sounded exactly like their mother.

He heard his mother laughing, and then he heard something else.

For a dizzying moment, Davison thought he heard both his mother *and* his father behind him, laughing in collusion, watching with great amusement as he acted out the script they had written for him so long ago.

Reaching for the Sun

The air was chill, but not cold. Morning dew shone on the dunes like a sheet of translucent silk.

Horace sat up and regarded the rabbit prints, like a design on the silk, as they led over the ridge.

Tomorrow morning, when the rabbit came back, in the eerie twilight between dew set and sunrise, he'd put a bullet in that bunny and have himself some real breakfast. Roasted rabbit breakfast.

The thought of it made his empty stomach rumble. He knew what food was left in his pack and he didn't even want to look at it. Crushed crackers and a handful of greenish salted meat, the only leftovers from the camp he raided last week. They must have been hunters or soldiers or something, because the camp was littered with empty metal bullet cartridges and slivers of bone, along with the crackers and meat that they'd either forgotten or thrown out. Horace hated eating that stinking, salted meat, but had choked some down for the protein. It had given him the runs—dangerous runs, because he had been so empty to begin with.

He wished one of those soldiers would happen on by right about now—he'd have himself some soldier stew. With crackers.

Either that, or they'd arrest him. One way or another, Horace would get himself a meal, and that's what he needed most.

Soldiering had seemed like a good idea when he put his X on the line. They gave him all new clothes and fed him regular. But when he signed up, he didn't know about the war going on, and as his tent mates started polishing up their rifles and talking about killing, that rabbity feeling came over Horace again, and he knew. He talked the talk, and he buddied around with them as long as the tent kept him dry and the cot kept him off the ground and the hot food kept flowing into his stomach and the pay was regular. But when they started packing up to move out, Horace beat them all to it.

It was a trick he had learned. Stay away from trouble. Keep one step ahead of it. War was trouble. So was desertion, but hell, it wasn't nearly so bad as war.

Besides. War was wrong.

He'd avoided soldiers after that. They weren't hard to avoid, them and their wagons and their horses all jangled and rattled, and they wore those uniforms as though they were proud to. They were bigger than life, and when Horace peered around the corners of buildings, or through the blinds of windows at wagons full of them, he remembered the pride he had felt in being a representative of the United States of America. Inwardly he envied them and outwardly he scoffed and made fun of them.

He'd like to have been the type of person who could find it in his soul to give his life for his country, but he wasn't that type of person. He just wasn't, and wanting it wasn't going to make it so.

It would be all right with him if a whole damned regiment came over that dune right about now, arrested him, threw him in the stockade and brought him a big, steaming bowl of anything and about six gallons of water.

But no soldier was likely to come by here. Nobody was likely to come by at all. If Horace were smart, he'd head on back to town, tail between his legs, and take his licks. He was a bad man and he'd done bad things, and if he owned up to it, if he repented like the preacher said, maybe he could balance the ledger and live long.

But Horace wasn't smart, and he knew it, and he also knew that like as not, a coyote would fight a buzzard for his sorry remains within the next day or so.

Unless he bagged himself that rabbit.

He watched the line of shade recede as the sun rose, the dew evaporating into a thin mist in its wake. The mist tarried for the briefest of moments like the ghost of Horace's hopes, and then vanished.

Freedom had become Horace's prison from the moment he'd wandered away from his daddy's house. He did whatever it took to maintain that freedom, but never quite got the hang of it. He was free, but he was afraid of everything. He lived his life as if someone was going to catch him, recognize him, shoot him or arrest him at any moment. And like as not, someone was trying to. If it wasn't some woman, then it was some store owner, or some rancher, or some banker, or some buddy or some sheriff. He couldn't keep a wife, he couldn't keep a job, he was too afraid of being held down. So he took women, and he took money and he took food and he lied, cheated and stole his way through the years.

In retrospect, lying here dying on this heap of sand, all that seemed unnecessary. Could he have been different? Could his life have been different? Could he have been a good man, a solid man, a responsible man? Could he have stuck to a solid code, like his pa tried to teach him, like the Army tried to teach him, like that purty woman tried to teach him?

He wasn't sure what that even meant.

Getcherass up and turn yourself in. That's a start.

No can do.

Then let's not waste time regretting things.

Too soon, the sun was full upon him and he was too dry to even sweat, thanks to that squishy meat and all the moisture his innards had required to expel it.

He emptied the pack onto the sand and put it over his head, but it acted like an oven instead of shade. His tongue swelled, hot and dry, until his mouth could no longer contain it.

So he lay in the sand, the empty canvas over his head to keep his tongue from sunburning, and he began to scheme about the rabbit.

It was brown and white, this rabbit, a little gray with age, and its beard had a little cast of red to it. A rogue rabbit, it never had fit in, always roamed alone, raping, pillaging, never apologizing, never returning, always leaving, always running, running—running out of places to hide.

It needed to be dead, that rabbit.

Maybe some good could be realized from its death; certainly, no good had come from its life.

Horace could eat it. He could eat it and appreciate it and respect it then. People would continue to talk for years, but perhaps in this, its final act, some redemption could be found for its wretched life.

Blindly, Horace felt around the sand for his gun, for soon the stupid rabbit would come by, and he couldn't miss its visit. He wouldn't survive another day—hell, he was only staying here this extra day to kill the damned thing and keep it from doing more damage.

And then he'd have himself a meal.

The gunmetal was hot, and he drew it into his own shade, a weak hand on the grip, a finger on the trigger. He rested from the extraordinary exertion, blinking dry eyes that could no longer see—smacking cracked lips over a sand-coated tongue. He'd be ready when that rabbit came by, that thieving murderous damned rodent. That's what his father had called him: murderous, thieving evil thing, and the rabbit had run. "Broke your mother's heart," his father had said. "She died because of you."

But it wasn't Horace's fault. He had tried. He'd tried to be what she wanted him to be, he'd tried so hard he damned near died hisownself. He almost drowned in his own juices trying to work in a store, being nice to the customers, being nice to the boss's wife, being nice to the owner, accepting a ridiculously insufficient wage. He tried, every day, Mama, he tried, he just couldn't do it, couldn't you see, couldn't you ever see that it just wasn't in him to reach for whatever loftiness she wanted him to grab hold of?

She wanted him to become something foreign, something that it just wasn't him. He was a rabbit, he was. He was a murderous, thieving, evil thing, and she wanted him to be young and beautiful, good and gracious, handsome and clean.

Holy.

But all he ever really wanted to do was to kill that damned rabbit. He needed to eat that rabbit. *C'mere, bunny, let me feel your soft fur.*

Soft, soft like his mother's hair.

She'd hold him on her lap and pet him, and croon to him. She, always frail, always fragile, wore those simple little dresses with flowers on them. She spoke softly and sweetly to him, he was her angel, he was her favorite little man, he was the one who would carry on the family pride. His eyes would close, and he'd purr inside like a kitten. He loved her so much; he wanted to do whatever she wanted him to do.

But he couldn't. He grew up, and as he did so, other things interested him, things she didn't like, didn't want, didn't approve of, so he hid them. He was always hiding things in his compartmentalized warren of a life, trying to be her darling when he was with her, and his true self when he was with his outlaw friends. He was too curious, too eager, too interested in other things, things that he was sure she didn't know about. And then he was too lazy, too irresponsible and too resentful. He felt rebellious about everything his parents had, wanted, or cared for. Particularly his own vile existence. It didn't take long for his own interests and habits to disgust him, but he was curiously powerless to help himself. To stop himself.

Like he was curiously powerless to turn himself in to the sheriff. Or the Army. Or anybody right now. Right now.

Go do it, do a decent thing for once in your life.

Not a chance.

It almost killed Horace when his mother died, because he knew his father spoke the truth. She died of a broken heart, because of the bad man he'd become—he'd never been able to hide it from her, not when he was young, and not when he became notorious—and now he was dying of a broken soul in atonement.

He couldn't even muster the energy for a prayer.

He remembered the last time he prayed. Maybe it was the only time in his life he had ever done a righteous thing, praying that one prayer. He couldn't remember any other time he had ever lifted his eyes to God. But when he saw those two little girls, he couldn't help himself.

He'd had his way with a willing young lass, and continued to come around and avail himself of her until her belly grew undeniable. Then, true to his nature, he skittered off into the brush, doing whatever he knew how to do, until life brought him back around into her town. He remembered her soft, sweet flesh, he remembered being connected up with the nature of things every time he was inside her, and he wanted more of that, so he dropped on by.

The baby was just walking when he came into her parlor, and foolish woman that she was, she greeted him with open arms and parted legs and soon that belly was growing again. This time he took off for good, until about a dozen years later when he happened in on the same town, and he spied on them.

There was something wrong with that woman, that woman who had been his bedmate, because she never took a real man for a husband. She raised those two little girls on her own, and the one and only time Horace prayed for all his worthless soul had in him, was when he saw those little girls dressed up for church and he saw that they were made precisely in the image of his mother. Regrets choked in the back of his throat as he looked at them, all white lace and yellow ribbons and he lifted his eyes to the harsh dry sky and said, "Please God, make them like my mother and not like me."

And then the woman, their mother, looking still youngish and lovely, followed them out of the house, and Horace ached for her, ached for himself, ached for a normal life, ached to be a man, a citizen, a taxpayer.

Those feelings scared him more than the sight of his mother in those granddaughters of hers, and he scampered away.

It got down to that damned love thing, he thought as he hightailed it out of town. When the mother of those girls told him she loved him, he thought the heavens had opened up and God had smiled down on him, because there just wasn't anything better than eating eggs with biscuits and gravy and drinking strong coffee the morning after lying with her. But that love feeling was just an illusion. The truth of love was that it was made of steel bands. Chains. Barbed wire. It promises to feel good in order to lure you in. The pretty woman is the bait, the hunger makes you bite. And then you're hooked. And good as dead, drowning daily, inch by inch, in social and domestic niceness.

The life steamed out of Horace's desiccated body as the barrel of the gun nestled right into that soft gray-brown fur. Going to make a nice rabbit stew, he said, or thought he said, just before he mustered the last of his strength.

Worthless rodent. Kill it.

He held the barrel of the gun tight against that bunny's fur and actually pushed hard against his chin to get enough leverage to pull the trigger and send the evil thing straight to hell.

~ ~ ~

The air was chill but not cold. Morning dew shone on the dunes like a sheet of translucent silk. A lone jackrabbit stood at the top of the hill surveying the remnants of the coyote's meal.

A shadow passed overhead, and the rabbit hopped up the hill, away from where the buzzards would soon land, his prints leaving a pattern on the dewy sand like flowers on silk.

The Sacrificed One

Sam pulled the garbage can out of its nook at the side of the house, and wearing his pajamas, robe and slippers, did his weekly Sunday night duty by wheeling the heavy thing out to the curb. He situated it just right so that the garbage truck could pick it up with its giant tongs, and as he turned back to shuffle back to the house, saw a man sitting cross-legged on the edge of the lawn.

"Hello?" he said, not wanting to walk across the lawn and get his slippers wet in the dew but needing to find out what someone was doing there.

The man was facing the street, his head down, and his shoulders shook ever so slightly, as if he were crying.

Sam didn't need a drunk crying on his lawn. Whoever he was, he could do his crying somewhere else. "Hey, pal," Sam said. "Might be time for you to go home."

The man wiped his face on his hands, then dragged his sleeve across his nose. He nodded, and stood up, shoulders stooped by the apparent weight of the world. He turned toward Sam, his face barely illuminated by the starlight and the light coming from Sam's draperied living room. "Can I show you something?" the man asked.

The question caught Sam off guard. The guy didn't sound drunk. "No," he said. "I'm in my pajamas. It's time for you to go home and get into yours."

"Come here," the guy said. "I just want to show you this thing."

"No, thanks," Sam said, intrigued in spite of himself.

"It's pretty interesting."

"Interesting enough to make you cry on my front lawn? Why would I want to see that?"

"Because you're a kind man."

Sam had all kinds of arguments to counter that statement, as if the guy knew whether he was kind or not, but in fact he was, and so he tightened the belt on his robe, walked down the driveway to the street and beckoned to him. "Okay," he said. "Hurry. My wife is waiting for me."

The man got up and met Sam in the street and reached inside his jacket.

Sam pulled back, afraid the guy was a lunatic or something with a gun, but to his surprise, the guy pulled out one of those old View-Master things.

"Hey, I remember those," Sam said. The guy, he noticed, though his face was shaded, was clean shaven and had a short haircut, was dressed cleanly with a new shirt tucked into clean jeans and a belt. He wore nice sneakers. This was no bum, no drunk. He was a man with a problem, and Sam, blessed in his life with few problems, could afford to help a guy out for a few minutes, whatever that meant.

"This is how you get rid of the worst memory of your life."

Sam walked slowly toward the guy, a little fear tickling the back of his neck. What did that guy mean he could get rid of a memory?

The one memory Sam had spent thirty years repressing burst from its carefully-crafted prison and engulfed him in the horror, the guilt, the shame of it. He still heard the thump as his father's car hit the child, the sudden silence in the car as he and his drunken friends realized what had happened, the sound of the old Pontiac as Sam floored it and ran like a coward from the body of the child left in the road.

He smelled the stink of rum and then the vomit as Charlie puked in the back seat, heard Joey's pleading to stop and go back, Good God, Sam, stop! Go back! You hit somebody. Not somebody, Sam said, a cat. It was a cat. It wasn't a cat, Joey yelled. *It was a little kid!*

Sam kept going, pulled the car into the carport at his parents' house, turned off the motor and threw the key he'd had made into the trash can. Then he cleaned the rum and taco vomit from the back seat and told his friends to go home and keep their mouths shut.

They did.

Sam burned with this memory until the day that little boy was buried, and then he built a fireproof box in his head and stuffed it all in there, all the sounds and smells and feelings of that night, slammed the door and put a big padlock on it, where it had remained until this very moment.

After the much-publicized funeral, the kid's parents divorced and moved away. Sam lost touch with Joey and Charlie after high school, and that was just as well.

He grew up, had a son of his own, and though the memory threatened to leak a little poison into his system when he saw his son at about 3 years old running around independently, he stuffed it down and worked hard to keep his boy safe. He knew he deserved for his son to die a terrible, needless death, but for some reason, the gods let him keep his own boy to watch to grow into a man. Where had that other little boy's parents been, letting him run into the street like that? They were the ones at fault, not him.

And now this man, this stranger, offers him a way to be rid of that memory? What was he about to finally pay for his youthful misdeed? Was he about to see his old childhood friends? Were there pictures of the parents of that little boy here, to torture him the way he had surely tortured them for their entire lives?

He didn't care. The very idea that he could be rid of this heavy burden, this tremendous weight that he now clearly saw that had colored his entire life, was so attractive that he would do anything—*anything*—to be rid of it.

He would do anything.

"To erase a memory, you must sacrifice a memory," the guy said, and handed Sam the viewer. "Choose wisely."

Sam's heart pounded in his ears. Slowly, he put the viewer up to his eyes and saw himself as a young boy, in his mother's arms. "Am I dying?" he asked as he clicked through the pictures. That could be the only explanation for this profoundly detailed slideshow of his life passing before him.

"No," the man said, but Sam did not look at him, so captivated was he by the three-dimensional memories flashing in front of him.

Pictures evoking memories of his childhood, his parents, his brother. Memories of vacations and school, and fights and friends and his first kiss. Memories of secret dreams and dying pets and the first taste of a cold beer on a hot day. Memories of his wedding and promotions at work and the birth of their son. Memories of the boy's first steps and first day of school and his college graduation. All his memories, flowing by with the slides.

It was overwhelming. Wonderful memories. Fabulous memories. Things he would never want to forget. Each one was a precious gem in his life. He didn't deserve to have such a successful, happy life after what he had done.

But I was just a kid, he rationalized again and again and again. A stupid teenager.

And then the picture of him in the hospital. This was kind of a weird memory in the midst of all the golden memories shown him. That had been a terrible time, being so very sick with leukemia, feeling terrible all the time, not being able to go out and play with his friends.

"This one!" he said. He handed the View-Master to the guy. "This is the one! I don't want that memory!"

"You're sure?" the man said. "You want to sacrifice this particular memory in order to erase the horrible memory you've been carrying around?"

"Of course I'm sure," Sam said, and handed the View-Master back. Getting rid of two bad memories in one fell swoop. What's not to like about that scenario?

A swirl of dizziness plowed into him, and darkness overtook his mind.

~ ~ ~

Sam came to slow awareness, first by the cramping in his gut and then the jangling in his nerve ends. He wiped the crust from his eyes and reached for the crumpled pack of cigarettes on the floor next to the bare mattress he slept on. Before he could get the cigarette lit, the cramping increased and he stumbled to his feet and barely made it to the toilet before the brown runny water that burned his ass poured out in a stream.

He relaxed on the toilet, lit the cigarette and took a long draw that made him cough until a wad of gray sputum landed on the floor between his bare feet.

Someone pounded on the door, and Sam's sphincter seized up.

"Hey, I'm coming in here with the police in one hour to throw your lazy ass out!"

Oh yeah, the landlord. Crap. At least he had an hour. What could he do in an hour?

Shower.

Sam turned on the shower and stepped in. There was the barest sliver of soap left in a glop on the side of the tub, so he used what he could to wash himself, trying to stand up straight, trying not to puke, feeling sicker than ever.

There was a shopping bag in the corner of the other room that the visiting nuns had brought, with new underwear, socks, a pair of jeans, a shirt, belt, toothbrush and paste, and a comb.

He dressed, put on his jacket and looked around the ugly room, then saw the old View-Master in the corner of the room. It was the only thing he had of any value. Kind of an antique. He picked it up, tucked it into his jacket, and walked out.

He needed something, but he didn't even know what anymore. He was sick of the dope, sick of kicking the dope, sick of doing the things he had to do in order to get the dope, in order to eat, in order to live, if you called this living. He was sick and tired of being sick and tired.

He stumbled down the street during the late afternoon, hookers and old cronies avoiding him. He'd burned each of them one too many times, and now there was nobody to help him when he needed it the most.

At the corner market, where the Italian lady had always given him day-old pastry or sometimes a little something more substantial, sometimes even the contents of the quarter compartment in her cash register. This time she looked at him with anger flashing in her eyes. "Get out of here, asshole," she said.

"What? What did I do?" It didn't matter. It could have been anything; he had done so much to so many.

"There's something wrong with you," she said. "Nobody ever taught you any compassion, you evil sonofabitch."

She was right. Sam backed out of the store, picked a direction and began walking.

Compassion. She was right. He had never learned compassion, at least he had no memory of anybody ever showing him any, never. He'd never shown compassion because he'd never felt any. His life was one shitty experience after another.

If only he could do it all again. If only he could go back in time and trade his life for another's. If only he had one single nice memory, something sweet that he could cling to, some time in his life where someone loved him enough to teach him to love others, to give him the tiniest bit of hope...

A faint recollection began to bleed through, as a man who had once stood up straight, who had lived a good life, who had money and family and the finer things. Something had happened, though, to that man, something from his past that came to haunt him, and he traded it all for a false peace of mind.

As night fell, Sam found himself on a vaguely familiar residential street. Exhausted, sick and starving, he half fell to a beautifully-manicured lawn, and there he sat, head in his hands. He had made poor choices in his life, and the more he contemplated them, the more he began to remember about a particular night just like this, and a selfish decision he had made.

Too bad. This was the end. He had made his decisions, lived his life, and now it was over. He could not go on.

The door to the house opened and a man emerged, wearing a bathrobe over pajamas. He wrestled with a garbage can and wheeled it to the street.

And Sam knew what to do.

Tight Corners

"Terrance?" The indistinct female voice was shrouded in static.

"Hello?" Terrance Stillman held the cell phone to his right ear and covered his left with his hand. "Hello?" His cell service was the shits, and in the Sink Hole bar, he could barely even hear the guy on the next barstool. "Hello? Hold on."

He took the phone into the men's room, but two guys were crowding into a stall, and whatever they were up to, it wasn't conducive to a phone conversation with a woman, whoever she was. "Hold on," he said again, and exited the stinking toilet and threaded his way through the Friday night crowd toward the front door.

"Wait," he said, shouldering his way out. His love life had been on a losing streak lately, and he wanted to capitalize on any prospects.

The cold midnight air slapped him in the face after the smoky, steamy bar, and he breathed beer out in a plume. "Hello?" he said. "You still there?"

But all he got was static.

"Hello?" The line was still open. He checked the little antennas in the corner of his phone display, and the signal was plenty strong. She had to still be there. "Hey," he said. "Hi. You there?"

"Terrance," the voice came again, thready and far away.

"Where are you?" he asked. "You sound like you're in Antarctica or something."

"Help me, please."

"Who is this? Where are you?" Sobriety slapped him as hard as the frosty air had. "Hello? Who's there?" Static. "Hello?"

Then way in the midst of the static he heard her voice again. "Terrance," she said.

Disconnect.

"Hello? Hello?" But the phone was dead.

Terrance ended the call and then scrolled through the listed history, but it said his last phone call was from his office. This one hadn't registered on his system for some reason. He made a mental note to change cell service in the morning. Some woman was out there wanting him, and he couldn't get to her.

He went back into the humid bar. Perhaps some girl in there would be willing to salvage his deteriorating evening. And sure enough, within ten minutes, he was dancing hot and dirty with a drunken young thing, who let him run his hands all over her while she writhed and laughed, and later in his car, she gave him the best blow job he'd ever had.

The weekend was wasted with hangovers and football, and on Monday morning, his boss called him on the carpet. "Your numbers are down," he said. "I'm putting you on provisional probation. It costs us to have you occupy that desk, Stillman, and if you're not going to perform, we'll have to get someone to sit there who will. This is not a social club where you can hang at the water cooler all day long."

Just then, his cell phone rang in his pocket. Bad timing. He pulled it out and turned it off.

"See?" the boss said, "Your priorities suck." He pointed at Terrance. "No personal calls on my time." Then he slid a paper-clipped bundle of sheets across the desk. "Here are your sales stats. You've got two weeks to bring them up to minimum, or you're outta here."

Terrance nodded. He didn't need to lose his job. Not now. Not ever, really, but especially not now. He had too much debt with credit cards, the new car and the nice apartment. This was a good job with sky-high potential, if only he could keep himself in order. He better not piss it away. "Yes, sir," he said. "Sorry. I'll improve. I promise."

"Yeah, yeah, I've heard it all before," the boss said, then dismissed him with a wave of his hand.

Terrance was certain the man *had* heard it all before, and he felt like a schmuck for being such a cliché. He held his resolve in his fist along with his stats and went back to his cube to get some real work done.

And he did. By the end of the day, Terrance was exhausted but pleased. The boss would be happy about extending the second chance. In two weeks, he was going to smoke all the rest of the guys in the pen. He'd make more sales than all of them combined, and he had a rockin' good start on it.

He went home, fixed himself a dry martini and turned on the television to watch the news.

Then he remembered his cell call while in the boss's office. He shucked his shoes and took the phone from his pocket and turned it on. There were four voice messages. They were all the same. Just static. On the last one, he thought he heard that voice again, faintly, but he wasn't sure. He listened over and over again but couldn't make it out. He erased the messages.

"Terrance, please help me," she had said. Who the hell could that be? He ran through a mental Rolodex of women who had his cell number. There weren't many. He kept on the move, contact-wise, changing his number every so often, just in case any of his little swimmers found the mother lode so to speak. He didn't need any entanglements of the parental sort, or any other sort. His mother was dead, his sister lived with her loser husband in the next town. He didn't have any ex-wives, and no ex-girlfriends who would call him for help. Not that he was proud of that, but it simplified things. He didn't want any woman to tell him how many martinis he could drink in an evening.

He set the phone on the coffee table. Maybe she'd call again, and they'd get a better connection. He drained his martini and fixed himself another. He'd like to help her if he could. He really would.

That week, Terrance kept his nose down and his mind on the job, and at the end of the week, his boss made a point to come by his cube and give him a thumb's up. Terrance was pleased, and proud of his performance. His job was safe for another week at least. He felt like celebrating.

The Sink Hole, or the Hole, as it was called, was the office hangout, with good, loud music and hot girls on Friday nights, so after work, he and a few coworkers loosened their ties and went out. Terrance started a credit card tab and bought rounds since his sales success was the highest for the week.

Just before midnight, that same girl showed up, the one with the oral expertise, and she grabbed a tipsy Terrance off his bar stool and dragged him through the crowd to the dance floor, where they got hot and sweaty and very horny. By the end of the third song, they were rubbing up against each other in a way that would have even offended a sober Terrance, but he had his hands full of her and he wasn't about to let go.

"Let's go outside," she said, her eyes full of twinkle and her blouse full of boobs. "I think you're very cute."

"I am extremely cute," he responded, and followed her out into the winter air. The chill felt good on their overheated bodies, and Terrance took her to his car. He got in the driver's seat while she climbed in the passenger side, then he grabbed her and unzipped his pants with one hand while he smashed her mouth against his with his other hand on the back of her head.

She pulled away from him. "Not here," she said.

"Not here?" he said, his alcohol-saturated brain not quite tracking.

"No," she said, looking around as if hiding from someone. "Not tonight. Let's go somewhere else."

His hard on was making a lot more sense than she was, so he slipped his key in the ignition and turned it over. He pulled slowly and carefully out of the parking lot and then stomped it, leaving a chirp of rubber on the road. She squealed, and he liked both sounds. He liked them a lot. He liked feisty women, hot cars, and dry martinis, and tonight he was on a roll.

And she had her hand in his pants while he drove.

"I know a place," she said.

"Just keep doing that," he said.

She did and he drove.

Five minutes later, he pulled into a state campground, parked, turned off the lights, and then reclined the seat and raised the steering wheel out of her way. She did her magic—good god, where did she learn to do that thing with her tongue?—and he lay back and concentrated. She was fabulous. When he was finished, he got her out of her panties amid much giggling, and they tumbled into the small back seat, where he tried, but was unable to do much for her. She didn't seem to care. She liked his company, and he certainly liked hers.

"You better take me back to the Hole," she said, but Terrance was warm and cozy and didn't want to move. His eyelids felt heavy, and his arms heavier. He just wanted to lie on top of her, his face against those sweet firm boobs and sleep the rest of his life away. "C'mon, Terrance," she said, jiggling him. "It's late. I'm getting cold."

"Okay," he said, and dragged himself into a sitting position. He didn't feel very good, but if she was going to be like that, he was just as well to be rid of her. In fact, she was starting to sound a little bitchy. The more he thought about it, as he climbed back into the driver's seat, the more he couldn't wait to dump her ass back at the bar.

He fired up the engine and threw it into reverse, catching her halfway between the back seat and the front seat. "Honey, wait," she said, but that only irritated him, and he spun the wheel, slammed it into gear and stomped it.

She fell back into the back seat. "Ow," she said. "Hey, come on, that was mean."

He didn't want to hear it. He floored it, and the gigantic engine in the car he loved roared. He relished the acceleration as the speed pushed him back into his seat. "Please slow down," she whined from the back seat.

"Shut the fuck up," he said, just as he came too fast around a corner. The tires lost traction on a patch of black ice, the car slid sideways, and though he desperately tried to control it by jerking on the wheel and slamming on the brakes, the auto left the road and rolled twice before smashing into a tree.

When Terrance came to, he was outside the car, though he had no memory of getting there. A front wheel on the upside-down car still slowly spun, and steam rose from its caved in hood.

Terrance checked himself over and found nothing to be permanently damaged. Nothing broken. Perhaps a few bruises, but he'd live.

The car, however, was a mess. His cell phone was in his pocket; he could call the police. He should call an ambulance. He didn't hear anything from the girl in the back seat.

But then he already had one DUI pending. If he got another, he'd lose his license. He could go to jail and kiss his job and apartment goodbye.

"Terrance?" he heard the soft groan come from the wreck.

He could walk back to the bar and claim that the car had been stolen.

"Terrance? Please help me." He looked toward the rear end. It had been flattened by the giant sequoia that had stopped them. He peered into what used to be the back seat, and realized there was no way anybody was going to survive that and be right. He'd be doing her a favor.

"Terrance?" the voice was softer, fainter.

He brushed off his suit and started walking.

Vivid Dreams

"These sleep aids have some side effects," the doctor said as he wrote on a little white pad. "Take one only when you absolutely need it."

"What kind of side effects?" Constance nervously twisted the white sheet in her arthritic hands, ignoring the pain.

"The most common complaint is strange, very vivid dreams."

"Oh, I don't mind that."

"It's a narcotic, so I'll leave this at the nurses' station." The doctor ripped the prescription from the pad and stood up. "If this doesn't do the trick for you, let the nurses know."

"Thank you," Constance said. She didn't like pills and didn't want to take a sleeping pill, but the pain in her legs was so severe these days that nothing they gave her settled it down. She hadn't slept a night through for months. The idea of falling softly to sleep and waking refreshed to a new day of pain in her crippled legs was so attractive that she wanted one of the magic pills immediately. She didn't want to have to wait for the prescription to be filled, but she knew that patience was a virtue.

"I don't like him," Nina said from her bed on the other side of the room. "He's my doctor too, but he's not long on bedside manner."

"I don't have to love him," Constance said. "If he can find me a solid night's sleep, I'll be forever in his debt."

Nina snorted.

Soon, the nurse came in with Constance's dose of pain meds, which lightened her mood and made living in this wretched nursing home more tolerable, but did virtually nothing for her twisted, aching legs.

Her day went by as all days before, and she assumed, all days until her death, with a sponge bath, bed linen change, the burly attendant putting her on the commode and helping to clean herself afterward, a game or two of cribbage with Nina while they were both up in their chairs.

Then lunch, a nap, and an hour of some stupid romance book on tape that the church ladies brought in, then television until the nurse turned all the lights out and Constance was left to suppress her moans of pain all night long until daylight softened the windowsills, and the routine started all over again.

But not tonight. Tonight, after dinner, the nurse brought a new yellow pill, the one that the doctor had prescribed, and Constance eagerly gobbled it down, then lay back and waited for those mysterious, vivid dreams that would take her out of pain and into the sheer joy of slumber.

When she opened her eyes, she was on a hill, overlooking the sleeping city. The small, misshapen moon shone high above. Constance took a step, and then another. She could walk! Her legs were as long and strong and straight as when she had been a teenager, running on the track for her old high school team. The night was balmy, and her favorite little yellow cotton sundress felt perfect.

She tested her feet and legs out, running around in a circle, and then as her confidence built, she ran down the street. The only sounds she could hear were her old, favorite tennis shoes slapping moist pavement, and her breath as it came effortlessly in and out of her lungs.

What a glorious feeling, to run again, to run as fast as she could, until she could barely catch her breath. Then she slowed and stopped, hands on her knees, bent over to stave off the stitch in her side. Her hands looked like the hands of a young person, fingers straight, skin clear, not painfully twisted with arthritis, thin-skinned with blue veins popping out of liver-spotted skin.

She was young again!

"Hello."

Constance straightened up and saw a little girl leaning against the trunk of a big tree. "Hello."

"Want to have some fun?"

Fun! Constance wasn't sure she knew what fun was any more. "Sure."

"Let's go!" The little one took off, sprinting down the street, and Constance took off after her, thrilled to be quick, agile, and able to keep up.

They ran for what seemed like miles, Constance luxuriating in the feel of the wind blowing through her long, red hair, perspiration cooling on her skin.

The younger girl stopped in front of a vaguely familiar building, long and low, with many windows. "Shhh," she said, then waved Constance to follow.

They walked quickly and quietly through the dewy grass and then behind a series of bushes, to peer into the darkened rooms.

Constance, stunned to paralysis by the image of her young face reflected in the window, couldn't see beyond the glass to look inside until the younger girl punched her on the shoulder. "See?" she asked.

Constance brought her hands up around her face to shield out the moonlight and she saw two hospital beds in the room. Slowly, she recognized the little figurines on one bedside table, the cheap pictures on the wall, the robe hanging over the foot of the bed.

"Not that one," the girl said. "This one, over here."

Tiny Nina seemed lost in the enormous bed, sleeping soundly with her mouth open. Constance felt a rush of affection for her roommate that she hadn't felt before.

This was all so very weird.

"Let's kill her," the girl said.

"What!?" Constance awoke with a start, and it was morning.

She had slept through the night for the first time in years, and she felt wonderful. Even the pain in her legs wasn't as severe as usual.

Those pills were indeed magical, vivid dreams and all. She could definitely put up with vivid dreams of youth and health and vitality.

That evening, she told Sally, her favorite nurse, that she wanted another of her sleeping pills, as the one the previous night had done her so well. Sally frowned, and read the label, striking terror into Constance's heart. What the hell did they care if she got addicted to some stupid drug? She was old and sick and in pain and would die soon anyway. Sooner than later, if she had anything to say about it. This was no way to live, and if a good night's sleep with strange, vivid dreams was all she had to live for, they should not deprive her of that.

"Please?" she asked in a tiny voice, inwardly furious that she had to beg for something that should be her right to take.

Sally shook one out of the bottle into her hand and handed her a glass of water.

Constance pulled her covers up and waited eagerly for sleep to take her to the land of health and vigor.

"Hi," the girl said when Constance arrived back on top of the same hill. "Ready to go for a run?"

"Yes!" Constance said, and they took off down the hill, flying like the wind.

Soon, she was out of breath, and they stood again in front of the familiar building, the nursing home. "This way," the girl said, and they walked through the foundation shrubbery on the north side. "This room."

They both peered into the room, and Constance saw old Esther McCoy in her bed, a line of spittle attached from her lower lip to the pillow. Old Esther spent her days in her wheelchair, bent over so her head rested on her knees, moaning.

"Let's kill her," the girl said, and Constance believed that there could be no greater act of mercy.

"Okay," she said, and then in the strange way of dreams, they were in the old woman's room.

"Put a pillow over her face," the girl said, and Constance did as she was told.

The old woman put up no fight at all. It was as if she were on the brink of death anyway – as she surely had been for months.

"Good." The girl nodded her approval as Constance put the pillow back where it belonged, and just like that, Constance awoke to Sunday morning, and time to get ready for a wheelchair ride to the little chapel.

The first thing the minister said was that prayers needed to be said for Sister Esther McCoy, who had passed in the night.

Constance felt the flush of shame, and she dared not look around, lest everyone in the chapel see the guilt on her face. She heard nothing else for the entire sermon.

Just a dream, correct? It was all just a dream. Strange, vivid dreams, the doctor had said. Surely this was all just a huge coincidence.

Still, that night, she asked Sally for another sleeping pill.

"Those are addictive, honey," Sally said.

"So what?" Constance snapped. "You deny an old woman a good night's sleep because of some stupid fear that I might get addicted to it? *You* try being stuck here in this bed with these legs and see how well *you* sleep the night through."

Hurt, Sally left the room and silently brought her back a pill and a glass of water.

The little girl was at the same place, and without asking, Constance knew where they were headed when they began to run. The night air filled her lungs with freshness and joy, and when they arrived back at the nursing home, she felt none of the remorse at the passing of old lady McCoy that she had in the chapel that morning.

"Not me again," Constance said. "It's your turn."

"Okay," the girl said, and then they were in the room of Mr. Miner, the old railroad engineer. Blind, deaf and of no use to himself or anyone else, the girl picked up the pillow and held it down over his face.

As with Mrs. McCoy, he put up no struggle whatsoever, and soon the deed was done.

And it was morning.

"Did you hear?" Nina asked. "Philip Miner passed in the night."

"It's about time," Constance said.

"I agree."

After three nights of good, sound sleep, Constance felt good enough to be helped into a wheelchair go to the smelly cafeteria for lunch, the first time she had made an appearance there in years. Kate, the aid with all the tattoos, wheeled her in and found her a place to sit at a table with other ladies who were younger, or at least more ambulatory. Everyone seemed glad to have Constance join them, but she was not up for small talk, she was looking around the room to see who might be the next candidate to be put out of his or her misery.

She saw several.

That night, she asked for her pill and countered Sally's hesitation with a stern look. She was going to take no crap about it, and Sally complied. Constance knew a note would be made in her chart, but she didn't give a shit.

She and the little girl ran through the night. Soon they were back at the nursing home, drawn there as if by a magnet. The little girl navigated them back to her own room.

"That one," she said.

"That's Nina," Constance said. "She's still full of life."

"She's not," the girl said. "Let's kill her."

"You do it," Constance said. "If she's your choice, then you have to do it. I can't, because she's my friend."

"That's the job of a good friend," the girl said. "You're her friend, and that's why you have to do it."

"No." Constance was adamant. "You have to do it."

"I can't. And it must be done. Come on."

They entered the room through dream magic, and a moment later, Constance stood over her friend's bed. She looked at the girl and saw a greedy eagerness on her face. "I'll miss her," Constance said.

"*Do it,*" the girl commanded.

Reluctantly, Constance picked up a pillow and approached her old friend's bedside. Nina slept quietly and peacefully, but as the pillow came down, she opened her eyes and looked Constance in the face.

Did she nod, just before the pillow snuffed out her air?

There was more fight in Nina than in the others, but not all that much.

The girl, standing behind her, laughed and then just as Nina gave up her ghost, the girl sighed. "Yes," she said quietly.

In the end, Constance knew that she had done her old friend a favor, just as the girl had suggested.

But when she put the pillow back and turned around, the girl was gone.

She immediately awoke to commotion coming from the other side of her room. Before she could chase away the cobwebs of her dreams, attendants had wheeled Nina's bed from the room with Nina's lifeless body still in it.

Constance felt a pang of loneliness, as her companion of so many years had now gone. No telling what kind of roommate she'd get to replace her. One who played cribbage, she hoped.

The next night, Constance ran like the wind, but her little companion failed to show up and join her. She ran and ran until she thought her heart would burst with the exhilaration of it all, and when she awoke, Nina's family was there to clean out her personal belongings.

"Excuse me," Constance said, and Nina's eldest daughter, box in hand, turned around. "Might I have something to remember your mother by? We were such good friends."

The daughter looked down at the open box she carried. "Here," she said. "Here's a picture of Mom when she was younger." She picked out a small, framed photograph and handed it to Constance.

The photograph was of the young girl in Constance's dreams. Somehow, Constance was not at all surprised, only that in her final moments, Nina had been so treacherous as to manipulate Constance to do her bidding, and then left without offering Constance an escape route.

"But who's to take care of me?" she asked no one in particular.

"The nursing home," Nina's daughter said as she walked out. "That's why you're here."

"No! That's not what I mean!" Constance shouted. "I mean who will take *care* of me?"

But by that time, they had all gone and she was left alone with her pain.

Unrequited Loss

When the clock struck seven, the vicar roused himself from a nod, stood up and addressed the sanctuary. All the long, wooden pews were empty but for one lone soul in the second row. "It is a cold night," the vicar said to the person seated. "Much too cold for people to leave their cozy houses and firelit living rooms and come to this drafty chapel. I daresay it will be only you and me tonight."

The young man who sat in the second pew nodded.

"What say we forego the service, and you come back to my quarters for some hot tea?"

The man, his hands deep in the pockets of his black overcoat, shrugged, then gathered his long legs under him and stood up.

"I'll take your arm, if you don't mind," the vicar said. The younger man offered his hand to steady the creaky old preacher down the steps and out of the sanctuary. "A sermon needs a certain number of people to hear it," he said. "Otherwise, it falls empty onto the stones. I'd much prefer a pleasant chat on such a raw night." They left the candles to burn in their holders, in case someone came seeking shelter on this freezing night and walked through an old wooden door into a tiny but warm and well-appointed kitchen.

"Mrs. McAffrey put on the teapot before she left. Would you have a cup?"

The visitor shook his head no and pulled a chair out for the elderly man. Once settled, the vicar pulled the plug on an old jug instead of opening the tea jar, and when his guest fetched a pair of short glasses from the shelf, poured three fingers of an amber liquid into each.

"Now," the vicar said, as he settled back, drink in hand. He undid the button on his collar and pulled it away from his sagging neck, then eyed the younger man. "How do you happen to darken the doorstep of this failing old church on the coldest night in decades?"

"I'm looking for a story," the young man said, removing his wide-brim hat and placing it gently upon a peg. "I think you have one to tell." A lock of hair, so black it appeared blue in the pale lamplight, fell forward onto the man's forehead. He stared at the vicar with intensity, his eyes dark and focused. The vicar could not begin to hazard a guess as to the man's age; only that he was much younger than he, himself. But then so was everybody.

"A story." The vicar sipped his booze. "Make yourself at home," he said, waving at the little chair opposite him.

The younger man shrugged out of the overcoat and let it fall behind him onto the back of the kitchen chair. Under it, he wore a fine Shetland sweater and pair of tweed trousers. The man had money, obviously, and with the well-honed cleverness that came from running too poor a parish for too long a time, the vicar thought he'd better tell a damn good story if he was going to pull a week's wages from this well-heeled man's pocket. "What kind of a story would you like?"

"A story of redemption," came the reply, and the man picked up his drink and took a swallow.

Perhaps it was a trick of the yellowed light globe, the vicar thought, but the man looked familiar. "Have we met before?" he asked.

The man smiled and shook his head.

"Redemption, you say," the vicar said.

The man rocked back on two legs of the kitchen chair and nodded.

The wind outside picked up.

"Light some candles for us then, while I think," the old man said. "On nights like this, the electric is like to give out."

The man moved with grace and delicacy around the small room, putting a match to the wicks of half a dozen candles, then sat back down and gazed at the holy man with anticipation. "Whenever you're ready," he said.

"Are you in need of hope, my son?"

The man smiled and relaxed. "I am merely in the mood for a good story. I believe you have one to tell."

And the vicar did indeed have one.

"I myself have been redeemed," the vicar said. "I was a rounder and a bounder, and now I am a man of God."

"When *exactly* did you come to be a man of God?" The question came too quickly. Like a challenge.

Again, the vicar had that strange sense of familiarity. He had seen this man before, had known him, had enjoyed some type of intimacy with him some time in the past. Even, perhaps, in his dreams. "Are you the son of my sister?" he asked in a moment of disorientation. Then he countered himself. "No, of course not, no, he would be twice your age." And for all he knew, his sister never had a son. They'd lost touch decades ago. Yet another regret.

The man merely smiled and shook his head. "You were about to tell me…"

"Yes," the vicar said. "I serve the Lord."

"Oh?"

"The greatest gift a man could receive is the calling to serve."

"I imagine."

But the vicar was suspicious of this man's attentive concern. It seemed mocking. He was eager to change the subject. "Listen," he said. "Do you hear someone in the sanctuary?"

"No," the man replied, and set his chair back on all four legs with an authoritative thump. He leaned forward, his eyes greedy. "Tell me about your… your… come to Jesus."

"Were you sent by the archdiocese?"

"No," the man said, his face softening.

"Who, then? Who sent you to inquire of my faith?"

"A higher authority."

"Higher?"

The man nodded slowly, solemnly.

The vicar was certain he could hear singing. Was it coming from the chapel? Could he hear the choir? On this frigid night? No, it was impossible. Was it the angelic chorus? Did this man bring angels with him when he came to call on an old man in his dotage?

The vicar looked at the younger man seated across from him. Redemption, he'd said. Sent by a higher authority. "Then you know about me," he said.

The man nodded slowly, solemnly.

A howl of wind rattled the windows. The table lamp flickered twice, then went out.

The candles placed around the room threw wavering shadows on the younger man's face, on his intense eyes, and the vicar knew he was being called to account.

"Saint Peter?" he whispered. "Is it you who will judge me?"

"Confess to me your sins," the man said.

"Must I?"

"Isn't it time?"

It was. "I am a fraud," the old man said in an outpouring of confession. "I falsified my credentials. I am on the run from the law in Brazil. I was never ordained. I am in hiding. I have been in hiding for forty-four years."

The man's expression never changed. The vicar saw no understanding there, no forgiveness, no empathy.

The vicar felt desperate to explain himself. "But I've redeemed myself over those years," he said. "I've helped people. I've ministered to this parish like no priest has ever done. Ask anybody. Ask everybody. I have dedicated my life to the service of these people and their spiritual needs." He began to gasp. He felt his chest tighten. "I am a good man. I have become a good man, through the grace of God." Tears began to choke him. "Please, please, if you have an ounce of mercy in your soul, you will let an old man live out his remaining days in the comfort of this small parsonage and the love of his elderly parishioners. Please. I beg of you."

"Name one person you have helped."

"There have been so many. So many." But in his panic, his memory failed him.

"One. Name one."

He slipped from his chair, fell to his knees and grasped the young man's cold hands. "I beg of you." He buried his face in the young man's leg. Music swelled around him. He knew for certain he was hearing the song of angels and hoped that they were singing a song of mercy and forgiveness.

"From what were you running?" The man asked, giving no sign of clemency.

The old man wiped the tears from his face, gripped the table and stood up with arthritic difficulty. He drank down the last of the whiskey and sat again in his seat. There was no dignity in begging; he had to ask for his forgiveness with decorum. But the burden he had carried all these years finally felt lighter. Confession was good. Odd, that while he advocated the benefits of confession all these years, he had never availed himself of it. He never felt worthy.

"I killed a lout in a brawl over a cheap woman," he said. "I killed Eduardo Martinez. Shot him twice in the chest. It was many years ago. I ran from the law. I escaped by the skin of my teeth. I have paid for that sin with my dedication to service."

"What of that woman?"

"Lucinda. A barmaid. A whore. I, with my youthful lusts, thought I was in love with her. I killed my competitor for her affections. I was stupid."

"And you have never paid."

The vicar stared at the man for a long moment before responding. "I have paid with my very life," he said. "I have paid every day by enriching the lives of those around me. I have remained chaste. I have lived frugally. I have dedicated my life to the doing of good." He felt righteous anger begin to burble up. How dare this stranger question his motives? "I have done much more good with my life than would have been done had I sat for years in a Brazilian prison."

The younger man remained silent.

"Tell *that* to your higher authority," the vicar said.

The music swelled around him. He closed his eyes and listened to the voices. He could swear he heard the superb soprano voice of Ethel Sweeney. Could the choir be practicing? On such a night?

"Tonight is the anniversary of my mother's death," the young man said. "Forty-four years ago. She died of a broken heart."

The vicar looked with horror at the young man's face, saw the Brazilian eyes, hair, skin tone. Knew that he was not Saint Peter, but something worse. Someone far worse.

"Please leave me be," the vicar said.

"You've had too many years," the man said.

"Please go. I hurt no one by being here."

"You hurt everyone with your deception,"—the vicar waited to hear the word, the word that would tear his heart apart— "father."

There. It had been said.

"I knew nothing of you," the vicar whispered.

"Of course you knew."

Of course I knew.

The stranger's eyes flashed with disdain, with long-suppressed rage. "You had to have known. You ran like a rabbit, leaving her alone. She died, you know, she died a horrible death within weeks of your disappearance."

The vicar listened. The heavenly voice of Ethel Sweeney soared throughout the chapel. She was in particularly good form on this cold, strange night.

"What do you think you can do to me now that I haven't already done to myself?" The vicar asked.

Then he stopped.

Wait a minute.

"Within weeks, you say? She died within weeks?"

The young man nodded his head, and as he did so, the vicar saw the gray at his temples. Saw the essence of the beautiful Lucinda, his mother, in that handsome face. The vicar was filled with a longing, a grief so great he thought it would pool on the floor around his feet and rise up to drown him.

"What must I do?" he asked.

"You need do nothing more," the man said. And the impossibly adult unborn son of his long-dead lover faded until the vicar could see the candlelight through his chest, and a moment later, the vicar was alone.

But not alone. Never alone again.

He bowed his head to say a prayer, and when the clock struck seven, he twitched awake and opened his eyes to see the candlelit sanctuary filled with parishioners. Ethel Sweeney's final note still reverberated throughout the rafters.

A dark-haired stranger sat in the second pew, his wide-brim hat resting respectfully on his knees.

About the Author

Elizabeth Engstrom is the author of nineteen books, some fiction, some not. She is a former teacher, editor, and publisher, with a BA degree in English Literature, concentration in Creative Writing, and a Master of Arts in Applied Theology with a certificate in Pastoral Care. She lives in the Pacific Northwest with her husband, the legendary muskie fisherman Al Cratty, where she puts her pen to work for social justice and is always working on the next book. Find out more: www.elizabethengstrom.net

IFD Publishing Paperbacks

Novels:

Of Thimble and Threat, by Alan M. Clark
Baggage Check, by Elizabeth Engstrom
Bull's Labyrinth, by Eric Witchey
The Surgeon's Mate: A Dismemoir, by Alan M. Clark
Siren Promised, by Jeremy Robert Johnson and Alan M. Clark
Say Anything but Your Prayers, by Alan M. Clark
Candyland, by Elizabeth Engstrom
Apologies to the Cat's Meat Man, by Alan M. Clark
Lizzie Borden, by Elizabeth Engstrom
A Parliament of Crows, by Alan M. Clark
Lizard Wine, by Elizabeth Engstrom
The Door that Faced West, by Alan M. Clark
The Northwoods Chronicles, by Elizabeth Engstrom
The Prostitute's Price, by Alan M. Clark
The Assassin's Coin, by John Linwood Grant
13 Miller's Court, by Alan M. Clark and John Linwood Grant
Guys Named Bob, by Elizabeth Engstrom
Fallen Giants of the Points, by Alan M. Clark
The Itinerant, by Elizabeth Engstrom
York's Moon, by Elizabeth Engstrom
Night Birds, by Lisa Snellings and Alan M. Clark
The Witch of Wapping, by Rebecca J. Allred and Alan M. Clark

Collections:

Professor Witchey's Miracle Mood Cure, by Eric Witchey
Unrequited Loss, by Elizabeth Engstrom

Nonfiction:

How to Write a Sizzling Sex Scene, by Elizabeth Engstrom
Divorce by Grand Canyon, by Elizabeth Engstrom

IFD Publishing EBooks
(You can find the following titles at most distribution points for all ereading platforms.)

Novels:
The Prostitute's Price, by Alan M. Clark
The Assassin's Coin, by John Linwood Grant
13 Miller's Court, by Alan M. Clark and John Linwood Grant
Guys Named Bob, by Elizabeth Engstrom
Apologies to the Cat's Meat Man, by Alan M. Clark
Bull's Labyrinth, by Eric Witchey
The Surgeon's Mate: A Dismemoir, by Alan M. Clark
York's Moon, by Elizabeth Engstrom
Beyond the Serpent's Heart, by Eric Witchey
Lizzie Borden, by Elizabeth Engstrom
A Parliament of Crows, by Alan M. Clark
Lizard Wine, by Elizabeth Engstrom
Northwoods Chronicles, by Elizabeth Engstrom
Siren Promised, by Alan M. Clark and Jeremy Robert Johnson
To Kill a Common Loon, by Mitch Luckett
The Man in the Loon, by Mitch Luckett
Of Thimble and Threat, by Alan M. Clark
Jack the Ripper Victim Series: The Double Event (includes two novels from the series: *Of Thimble and Threat* and *Say Anything But Your Prayers*) by Alan M. Clark
Candyland, by Elizabeth Engstrom
The Blood of Father Time: Book 1, The New Cut, by Alan M. Clark, Stephen C. Merritt & Lorelei Shannon
The Blood of Father Time: Book 2, The Mystic Clan's Grand Plot, by Alan M. Clark, Stephen C. Merritt & Lorelei Shannon
How I Met My Alien Bitch Lover: Book 1 from the Sunny World Inquisition Daily Letter Archives, by Eric Witchey
Baggage Check, by Elizabeth Engstrom

D.D. Murphry, Secret Policeman, by Alan M. Clark & Elizabeth Massie
Black Leather, by Elizabeth Engstrom
Fallen Giants of the Points, by Alan M. Clark
The Itinerant, by Elizabeth Engstrom
Night Birds, by Lisa Snellings and Alan M. Clark
The Witch of Wapping, by Rebecca J. Allred and Alan M. Clark

Novelettes:
Mudlarks and the Silent Highwayman, by Alan M. Clark
The Tao of Flynn, by Eric Witchey
To Build a Boat, Listen to Trees, by Eric Witchey

Children's Illustrated:
The Christmas Thingy, by F. Paul Wilson. Illustrated by Alan M. Clark

Collections:
Suspicions, by Elizabeth Engstrom
Professor Witchey's Miracle Mood Cure, by Eric Witchey
Unrequited Loss, by Elizabeth Engstrom

Short Fiction:
"Brittle Bones and Old Rope," by Alan M. Clark
"Crosley," by Elizabeth Engstrom
"The Apple Sniper," by Eric Witchey

Nonfiction:
How to Write a Sizzling Sex Scene, by Elizabeth Engstrom
Divorce by Grand Canyon, by Elizabeth Engstrom

IFD Publishing Audio Books

Novels:
The Door That Faced West by Alan M. Clark, read by Charles Hinckley
Jack the Ripper Victim Series: Of Thimble and Threat, by Alan M. Clark, read by Alicia Rose
Jack the Ripper Victim Series: Say Anything But Your Prayers, by Alan M. Clark, read by Alicia Rose
Jack the Ripper Victim Series: The Double Event, by Alan M. Clark, read by Alicia Rose (includes two novels from the series: *Of Thimble and Threat* and *Say Anything But Your Prayers*)
A Parliament of Crows, by Alan M. Clark, read by Laura Jennings
A Brutal Chill in August, by Alan M. Clark, read by Alicia Rose
The Surgeon's Mate: A Dismemoir, by Alan M. Clark, read by Alan M. Clark
Apologies to the Cat's Meat Man, by Alan M. Clark, read by Alicia Rose
The Prostitute's Price, by Alan M. Clark, read by Alicia Rose
The Assassin's Coin, by John Linwood Grant, read by Alicia Rose
13 Miller's Court, by Alan M. Clark and John Linwood Grant, read by Alicia Rose

Novelettes:
Mudlarks and the Silent Highwayman, by Alan M. Clark, read by Alicia Rose

www.ifdpublishing.com